T0208808

COMMIE PINKO

Also by Janet Nichols Lynch

Wheel of Fire

My Beautiful Hippie

Racing California

Addicted to Her

Messed Up

Chest Pains

Peace is a Four-Letter Word

Where Words Leave Off Music Begins

Casey Wooster's Pet Care Service

Women Music Makers

American Music Makers

COMMIE PINKO

JANET NICHOLS LYNCH

COMMIE PINKO

iUniverse books may be ordered through booksellers or by contacting:

iUniverse
1663 Liberty Drive
Bloomington, IN 47403
www.iuniverse.com
1-800-Authors (1-800-288-4677)

Summary: During the McCarthy era, in Berkeley, California, fourteen-year-old Donna defends her physics professor father when he is suspoenaed by the House Un-American Activities Committee, forcing her between protestors and police in a dangerous conflict.

[1. Coming of age—Fiction.   2. McCarthyism—Fiction.   3.Cold War —Fiction.
4. Beat Generation—Fiction. 5.Teenage Pregnancy—Fiction.]

ISBN: 978-1-5320-1776-6 (sc)
ISBN: 978-1-5320-1779-7 (e)

Library of Congress Control Number: 2017902440

Print information available on the last page.

iUniverse rev. date: 02/20/2017

For the Lynch family

CHAPTER ONE

Every girl needs a crush, that one dreamboat in all the blue heavens who makes you squeeze your pillow at night and float through your days on pink clouds, your heart beating oh baby, oh baby, so you forget all the crummy things in life like algebra and the H-bomb.

My crush was Ritchie Valens. I already had worn out two copies of his hit single, "Donna"/"La Bamba." I *was* Donna, Ritchie's Donna. He was singing straight to me without even realizing it, and it was up to me to clue him in. Here was the setup. A) As president of the Official Ritchie Valens Fan Club, I would meet Ritchie. B) He would go ape over all the fans I got him, and he would ask me to be his steady. C) I would become Mrs. Ritchie Valens! Not right away, of course—I was only fourteen and he was eighteen—but eventually it just had to be. Fate, sealed with a kiss.

The first meeting of the Official Ritchie Valens Fan Club was held Friday, December 5, 1958, at 1550 Spruce Street, Berkeley, California, in my room. Well, it wasn't completely my room; I shared it with my big sis. My two best friends, Mary Lou Baines and Brenda Gardner, were there, and everything was running smooth as chocolate frosting, my favorite. We kicked off our saddle shoes and danced to "La Bamba" in our bobby socks, swinging each other so wildly that the braided rug slid clear across the hardwood floor. We flopped down on our bellies and swayed our feet to the pulsing sha-na-na beat of "Donna." As the needle scratched the center of the record, we screamed in unison "Ritchie!" and fake swooned, rolling over and over, giggling until our sides ached. I served the refreshments, Fritos and cherry Kool-Aid. Mary Lou, who volunteered to be treasurer, collected dues—a quarter each. I passed out the Official Ritchie Valens Fan Club membership cards, and that's when the trouble started.

Brenda turned her card over in her hand. "Why, this is just a cruddy ole index card. Who's gonna pay a whole quarter for something that costs a quarter of a penny? We need real membership cards, from the printer."

"Hey, I typed these! Typing is like printing," I pointed out. "Don't they look swell, Mary Lou?"

"Gee…they are kind of plain, but…" From behind her pink pointy-framed glasses, her squinty blue eyes shifted from Brenda to me. "I like the line where I sign my name."

"Perfectly straight! I used a ruler. Now, to snag more members, I say we each ask ten kids to be members and tell them to ask ten other friends, and then all of those kids can ask ten friends. You get the picture, like a chain letter, and then we'll have hundreds of members in a…" I snapped my fingers.

Brenda put on her sour lemon look. She was the pretty one, even with her mouth twisted up. She had waist-length wavy hair that I could never grow. It wasn't just her fab looks; Brenda had style. We were only freshmen, and already her mom let her wear lipstick. "Did you ever get those hundreds of letters you were supposed to get back from a chain letter?" she asked.

"I never got a single one!" exclaimed Mary Lou.

"That's because it doesn't work," said Brenda. "We need one of those slick ads in the back of *Sixteen,* and we gotta give our members more, like an eight-by-ten, autographed glossy of Ritchie. But before we make too many decisions, we gotta vote for officers."

"Hey, I'm president already!" I protested.

"You're the *founder* of the club," said Brenda. "That doesn't make you president."

"Mary Lou!" I howled.

"No offense, Donna, but Brenda does have awfully good ideas, and America is a democracy."

"We can use this cheap thing for ballots." Brenda ripped her Official Ritchie Valens Fan Club membership card into three jagged pieces. It might as well have been my heart. In a little movie in my mind, I saw

Brenda meeting Ritchie and *her* becoming Mrs. Ritchie Valens even though Ritchie never sang about Brenda at all.

A horn tooted from the driveway. Mary Lou jumped up and peered out the window. "Oh, it's my dad. We hafta go."

"Okey-dokey." Brenda laced up her shoes. "We'll vote for officers first thing next time. Meeting adjourned."

"I say 'meeting adjourned.'" I poked my chest with my finger.

"Ah, don't be a spoilsport," said Brenda.

"Spoilsport? Me? You're the one…"

"So long, Donna." Mary Lou wriggled her fingers apologetically. She hated taking sides. "Thanks for the Fritos and Kool-Aid."

As I followed my friends downstairs, I heard Brenda whisper to Mary Lou, "When I'm president, we'll have Cokes," knowing my mom didn't buy Coke because it rots your teeth.

"Good-bye, girls," called Mom, entering the foyer. Her bouffant beehive was freshly pinned and lacquered and she had put on her face, but she still wore her housedress and apron.

"Good-bye, Mrs. Kronenberger." Brenda held her skirt out as she curtsied. "Thank you for having us in."

Mom and I stepped out on the porch to wave as Mr. Baines backed out of the driveway.

"That Brenda Gardner has such nice manners," said Mom.

I fumed silently. Brenda always had tried to be the boss of Mary Lou and me, and I was fed up.

Mom leaned over the railing to peer down the street. "I wonder what's keeping your father. He knows we're having people in."

"Maybe he forgot," I said, as we went inside.

"I telephoned him on his lunch hour."

"Then he should be here any minute," I said hopefully. Dad forgot reminders, just like everything else. "I'll set up the bar so things will be ready when he gets here."

"That's a good girl." Mom cupped my face in her hands, her eyes very bright. She loved giving parties.

As I dashed across the living room to get the ice bucket, the front door slammed. There stood Alice like a matchstick about to burst into flame. She wore a tight black pencil skirt and a tight black turtleneck, with her pale face sticking out from under a black beret. One round eye glared at us, the other obscured by the sweeping bangs of her pixie cut. Her hair was actually blond like Mom's, but she had dyed it black to match her moods.

"Alice, you're home!" Mom exclaimed in amazement.

The telephone rang, and I answered it. "Kronenberger residence, Donna speaking."

"Let me talk to Leopold Kronenberger," said a gruff voice.

"He isn't home right now. May I take a message?"

"You bet you can, girlie. Tell him if he doesn't like it here, he can go live in Russia."

My heart beat faster. Something about the man's voice scared me. "Why would my dad go to Russia? He's from Austria!"

"Donna, who is it?" Mom's tone was hushed and strained.

The receiver clicked in my ear, and I returned it to its cradle. "What did the man mean, about Dad going to live in Russia?"

Mom didn't answer, her teeth gripping her lower lip.

The phone jangled.

"I'll get it this time." Alice stormed across the living room, fists pumping. "Hello?"

I was standing close enough to hear another angry voice. "Commie Pinko!"

"Ah, go crawl under the rock you came out from under." Alice slammed the receiver in the caller's ear.

"Where did you learn such language?" chided Mom.

Alice tilted back her head and laughed, a rare sight. "Bunch of ignoramuses."

"This must be about that article in the *Chronicle*," said Mom. "Did you see it, Alice?"

"I read it. Dad didn't do anything."

"What article?" I asked.

"Oh, it's nothing to concern yourself with, Donna." Mom patted my shoulder. "How about that ice you were getting?"

I just stood there, swinging the silver bucket. "What's a Commie Pinko?"

"A communist." Alice hooked her one visible eyebrow at me. "You've heard of them, right?"

"Is it like a Nazi?" Dad had been called a Nazi a bunch of times.

The telephone rang again. Mom's spine snapped straight, and she inhaled sharply.

"Cripes! I'll show them!" Alice reached out, but Mom was quicker. She gripped the receiver with white knuckles, holding it in place.

We listened to all seven rings, Mom wincing through them. I had never heard of not answering the telephone.

"I'll rip the damn cord out of the wall," threatened Alice.

Mom's sudden chirp of laughter sounded like a frightened canary. "What an idea!" As Alice stalked toward the stairs, Mom called after her. "Oh, sweetie, will you change into your lovely lavender chiffon?"

"Count me out of your little bourgeoisie cocktail party."

"But the Clifford Thomases will be here. With Stanley."

"Oh, Mother, please. Stanley Thomas is a business major. He'll probably be something square like a stockbroker." Alice snickered in a way that wasn't nice and loped upstairs.

Mom turned to me, her face crumpled into one of her I-just-don't-know-what-I'm-going-to-do-with-her looks. "What's wrong with a stockbroker? They make a very nice living."

"Search me." I went into the kitchen to fill the ice bucket, and Mom went upstairs to change. In the living room I arranged the bar, the way Dad and me liked it, ready for business. Usually I enjoyed party preparations, but now I had big worries and was just going through the motions.

By the time I got up to our room to dress for the party, Alice had vanished, having exited out the window and down the ivy trellis. I changed into a white blouse and my new black circle skirt. In neat little stitches, Mom had embroidered "La Bamba" and "Donna" in the center of the appliqued records. I redid my ponytail as high as it would go and tied a short white scarf over the rubber band, then fluffed up my bangs, which curled to the center of my forehead. I stared in the mirror and practiced the expression I would use when I met Ritchie for the first time, chin slightly tilted and eyes widened to a dreamy gaze.

The doorbell rang, and I heard raised voices and whoops of laughter. I hurried downstairs to greet my parents' guests.

"My, Donna, you're getting so tall," said Mrs. Deering.

I smiled shyly, not knowing what to say. Did grownups expect me to stop growing and be a midget for life? I slipped out the door and down the front steps. I spotted Dad trudging up Spruce Street, and I ran to meet him. His bulging leather briefcase slapped against his good leg. His other leg was stiff, which caused a limp that was more noticeable when he was tired. Alice and I used to goof around imitating his cockeyed gait until Mom told us to cut it out. Even though Dad had laughed, the teasing hurt his feelings.

His face stretched into a broad smile, which quickly faded when he looked into my face. He stopped dead in his tracks. "Donna girl, what is the problem?" he asked in his light German accent.

I crossed my arms. "We've got a houseful of people, for one thing, and you're not home yet!"

"Oh, that's right." He touched his fingertips to his brow. "Mommy's party is tonight! Is she in a dither about it?"

"Not much. She was getting worried about you."

"I tried calling to say I would be late, but I couldn't get anybody to pick up the telephone."

"Oh, was that you? We got so many calls this afternoon, I guess we got tired of answering them."

"What's this?" He reared back his chin.

I shrugged. "Just some men calling."

"Salesmen?"

I showed my open palms. "Beats me." I didn't want to tell Dad someone had called him a Commie Pinko. Instead, I started complaining about Brenda trying to take over the Official Ritchie Valens Fan Club. Dad listened quietly, his thick upper lip pursed and his bushy eyebrows rammed together.

"Well, well, Donna girl, just because we live in America doesn't mean everything must be decided by vote."

"It doesn't?" The pitch of my tone lifted hopefully.

"Not at all. Presidents of large American corporations are not elected, and quite often they are the founders."

"Really?"

"Does Ritchie sing to Brenda? Does he sing to Mary Lou? No! He sings to you, Donna. You tell Brenda you are the president, and that's the way it's going to be."

Somehow standing up to Brenda didn't seem that easy, but spilling the beans to Dad was a real relief. "If I showed you the membership cards I made, would you be honest if you think they look cheap?"

"Perfectly honest."

"Gee, thanks, Daddy." I put my arm around him and leaned against his big, soft body, which smelled of cigarettes and chalk dust.

As we turned into our driveway, Dr. Aldridge called, "About time you showed up, Leo." He was up on the porch talking to Dr. Tucker. Both of them were like Dad, physics professors at the University of California.

"Deering is threating to commandeer the bar," said Dr. Tucker. "The drinks will be watery."

"Not if he's pouring someone else's booze," joked Dad.

"Hello, Donna." Dr. Tucker smiled down at me as I mounted the steps. "I think your skirt is swell."

"Gee, thanks." I pointed to the embroidery on the records. "These are my two favorite songs."

"Oh, so you're not an Elvis fan?"

"No, sir. Alice and her friends went bonkers over Elvis, but he's too old for me."

"Is that so?" Dr. Tucker was the only young physicist. He was thin like Jack-Sprat-could-eat-no-fat, with a black beard and quick movements. He was my favorite professor because he didn't act like I was invisible.

When we got inside, Mom floated into Dad's arms, and he kissed her cheek. She was real swanky in her red strapless cocktail dress with the full, net skirt. They talked to each other with their eyes, Mom saying I'm so worried, and Dad replying never mind now, dear. She took his hat and overcoat to hang in the hall closet. "Darling, what kept you?" she asked, her bright smile reappearing. Without waiting for an answer, she chattered on about guests who had already arrived at the party. She lowered her voice to add, "Oh, and Edward Teller."

Dad reared back his head. "Who invited him?"

"Darling, he's a colleague!"

Behind the bar, Dad and I got down to business. He mixed the cocktails, while I put on the finishing touches: a maraschino cherry for a Manhattan, a green olive for a martini, and a pickled onion for a Gibson. Old-fashions were trickiest, with an orange slice, a lemon twist, and a maraschino cherry stuck on a plastic sword. When Dad had served all the guests, he made my usual, a Shirley Temple. He called it a Double Shirley because after I added a cherry, he plopped in a second.

The party got louder, smokier, and happier. The guests were professors Dad taught with and their wives; the members of the Faculty Wives Association Mom knew and their husbands; and the physicists Dad had worked with at the Lawrence Livermore Lab during the war. There was only one lady professor, a poet named Josephine Miles, tiny and crippled with arthritis. My parents' friends loved to argue and talk loudly over each other, but they never seemed to get mad. If they disagreed, they talked faster or made a joke, or jabbed the air and slurred their words because they had too many martinis. Then they lit more cigarettes and had more drinks and debated and laughed some more.

Finally, the subject that I had been listening for all evening caused my ears to perk up. "Spreading Communist propaganda in your courses now, are you Leo?" joked Dr. Tucker.

Dad took a long drag on his cigarette and blew out the smoke. "It's nothing worth mentioning."

"Oh no? The *Chronicle* thought it was," said Dr. Aldridge. "What exactly happened?"

Dad shook his head. "How do you call it? A tempest in a teapot." I could tell he didn't want to talk about it, especially with Dr. Aldridge, who often disagreed with him.

Mrs. Tucker grasped Dad's wrist and gazed into his eyes. She was young and pretty with thick eyeliner and tight, black beatnik clothes like Alice's. She gushed her words like an actress in a play. "I'd *adore* hearing the story straight from the *horse's* mouth, Leo."

"Very well. The topic of national security came up in class, and a heated discussion ensued. The next day, I added an extra credit question at the bottom of a quiz. Exactly how did I word it?" Dad lifted his eyes to the ceiling for a moment. "What are the dangers to a democracy of a national police organization, like the FBI, which operates secretly and is unresponsive to public criticism?"

Dr. Deering whistled. "How many extra credit points, Kronie?"

Dad batted smoke away with an irritated flutter of his hand. "Points? None whatsoever. Extra credit in the sense that it gave the students something more to think about."

"Hurrah," said Professor Miles, waving a shrimp on a toothpick like a pennant. Her fingers were stiff and slanted but her eyes flashed like lightning.

"Jolly good fun!" Dr. Tucker rubbed his hands together. "What sort of response did you get?"

"Most of the students were merely amused. A few offered sarcastic quips. Only a half dozen answered the question seriously."

Dr. Aldridge pursed his wide mouth into his bulldog scowl. "Aren't we supposed to be teaching physics?"

"Of course, Wally, but if a different topic arises in class discussion, I address it," replied Dad. "If students can't have an exchange of ideas at university, where can they?"

"Not at a cocktail party," Mrs. Tucker said drily. "They're too young."

"Then the stool pigeon was one of your own students!" Dr. Tucker noted.

Dad's bushy brows collided. "I know just the one."

Dr. Tucker shook his head in disgust. "Informing on his professor like a character out of Orwell's *Nineteen Eight-Four*."

"How futuristic," Mrs. Tucker commented blithely, fluttering her eyelashes.

"I'm afraid it's very much the present, Adele." The parentheses around Professor Miles' mouth deepened and her eyes grew black and solemn. "Do you know I have writer friends in Hollywood who can't get work? They're blacklisted!"

"Reckless behavior on your part, Leo," chided Dr. Aldridge. "You can expect the Americanism Educational League to pounce on this."

Dr. Tucker broke the tense silence with a slap on Dad's back. "By Jove, you've done it now, you gimpy old Nazi."

I popped my head under the crook of my father's elbow to confront Dr. Tucker. "My dad is not a Nazi! He's a citizen of the United States of America!"

"There, you see, Tuck? I'm perfectly safe. I've got my Donna to defend me. I'd like to see J. Edgar Hoover get past my good girl."

Dr. Aldridge puffed out his barrel chest. "All right, you fellows can laugh at Hoover if you'd like, but he's right, you know. If the commies are going to take us down, it won't be the Soviets. Our American institution will crumble from within."

Dr. Tucker shook his fist in Dad's face. "Oh, that's your game, is it, Kronie? Crumbling our American institution from within!" His face was so long and stern it took me a moment to realize he was still kidding around.

"Who ever heard of a communist Nazi?" asked the lady poet.

Grownup talk made my head swim. Now I was more confused than ever. I looked up into my father's face, splotchy and flushed. "Is a communist worse than a Nazi, Daddy?"

The party guests roared with laughter, and I felt hot with embarrassment. Grownups laughed when I least expected it.

Dr. Teller, who had been listening hard but not saying a word, held a weenie suspended on a toothpick for so long that cocktail sauce dripped onto his white shirt. I wondered how such a careless eater could be the father of the hydrogen bomb.

CHAPTER TWO

This was what I knew about communists. They lived in Russia. Some people said Soviet Union or USSR. It was all the same place. Communists were not free. They hated being free, and they were trying to get everybody in the world who was free to be communists. They could start World War III and drop an H-bomb on us, causing the world to come to an end.

I was thinking about this in a kind of daze, as I started walking to school Monday morning. I heard someone calling me from behind. It was Randy Greene, who lived next door. We had played together sometimes as little kids, when I couldn't have a real friend—a girl—over. Sometimes he would be Roy Rogers and I'd be Dale Evans. Or we'd swing from a rope tied to a tree branch, and Randy would say, "Me Tarzan, you Jane." The worst was when he put on his coonskin hat, we'd play Davy Crockett, and I had to be the bear.

When it's too embarrassing to talk to someone, you just pretend you don't see them. Now that we were in high school, Randy wanted to walk me to school every day. He even wanted to carry my books, which was a flat-out no. I walked faster.

"Hey, Donna! Didn't you hear me? Wait up!"

I stopped, only because I was forced to be nice to him. It was a matter of life or death. Literally, life or death. Randy came struggling along, lugging his big ole bari sax. He was so short that the popular boys like Rick Gorecki said, "What happened to you? Forget to grow?" and "You're so short, I bet you could commit suicide jumping off a curb."

I looked up at the sky. "Do you think Spudnik is watching us?"

"Do you mean *Sputnik?*"

"Oh, is that how you say it?" I had imagined a potato-shaped space ship with commies spying on me out the windshield. "Can the Russians see us walking down the street?"

"Lemme clue you, Donna. There aren't any cosmonauts in *Sputnik*. It's only about this big." Randy extended his arm like he was carrying a large beach ball. "It has four antennae that broadcasted radio pulses, until the transmitter batteries ran out, and it fell to earth in a fiery crash."

One thing about Randy: he knew stuff. I looked up at the sky again. "It's not up there anymore? Then why is everybody so worried about it?"

Randy poked at the bridge of his glasses. "We can't let the commies get ahead of us, not even in space."

"What do you think they do to commies—I mean communists—if they catch them in this country?"

"You can be a communist in America if you want. It's a free country."

"You can?"

"Uh-huh. But you might get blacklisted or deported or something."

Deported meant kicked out of the country. I didn't know what blacklisted meant, but the lady poet at the party made it sound horrible. I shook my head. "Holy moly."

"Are you worried about your dad, Donna?"

"No! I mean, yeah. Kind of."

"Governor Brown must not be."

"Hold it! You mean to tell me the governor of California knows about my dad's crummy little extra credit question?"

"Yes, ma'am. But he threw the complaint in the laps of the university's Board of Regents." Randy tilted his chin and sniffed me. "Is that perfume you're wearing, Donna?"

"To school?" I stepped away from him. He probably smelled the deodorant I had started using recently. Just the idea of having armpits was embarrassing enough, but here creepy Randy Greene smelled mine. "It must be my shampoo."

"Smells like perfume. Smells like eau de crazy for you." Randy fluttered his lashes, which were too long for a boy's. He was wearing a polka dotted bow tie. On popular guys they looked cool, but on oddballs they looked corny.

"How do you know that about the Board of Regents?"

"It was in the *Chronicle* this morning."

"Holy moly. Do you think my dad is in a lot of trouble?"

"Depends if he's a communist."

"He's not!"

"They could *prove* he's a communist or a fellow traveler even if he isn't."

"That makes no sense. How could they?"

"I don't know, but they do. You know what happened to the Rosenbergs." Randy set down his instrument case, squatted, and shook all over like he was getting electrocuted.

"They were spies!"

Randy picked up his case. "Maybe. Maybe not."

We passed a church with a fallout shelter sign and an arrow pointing to the basement. The sign was yellow with a black circle containing three yellow triangles pointing toward its center. These signs were all over Berkeley, guiding people to the shelters in case of a nuclear war. I thought if everyone ran into them at once, they would get pretty crowded. Randy's family had its own personal bomb shelter. It looked like a little white cement igloo in the center of their backyard. When my father saw it out the window of his second-story study, he got a big kick out of it. I didn't think it was a bit funny. I wanted our family to have one, too.

"How's your bomb shelter coming along, Randy?"

"My mom's still working on it, putting in blankets, canned goods, water. Yesterday she added Parcheesi and Monopoly."

"Nifty! Um...can I see it some time?"

"Mom says no. She says it's not a playhouse."

"I know that. I just want to have a look."

"Well, maybe I can sneak the key sometime."

"Gee, thanks." Randy was good for something, like maybe saving my life. I remembered I was supposed to recruit members for the Official Ritchie Valens Fan Club. Any warm body would do, so I asked Randy.

"Do I hafta like his music?"

"Are you kidding? Ritchie is fab! He's the best rock 'n' roll singer there is!"

"All rock 'n' roll is the same boring sha-na-na and do-wop-da-da. I dig jazz! Miles Davis, Charlie Parker, Dizzy Gillespie—those cats swing!"

"Never mind." We had reached school, and I turned away from Randy to go find Mary Lou and Brenda before the first bell.

"Wait, Donna. I'll join your club. That is…if you really want me to." He grabbed my arm and squeezed, fluttering his lashes again.

"It costs a quarter!" I exclaimed, flinging my arm away and looking around to make sure no one had seen Randy Greene touch me.

"Here." He pulled a quarter out of his pocket. When he gave it to me, his hand closed over mine, so that I had to jerk free and look around again. Randy snickered.

Every year in school we watched a movie called "Duck and Cover." In it, a cartoon turtle named Bert with a bow tie and hat pulls his head and limbs into his shell, while a man with a smooth, calm voice says, "If the atomic bomb comes and you do not know what to do, it could hurt you in different ways. It could knock you down or into a tree or wall." So in algebra that morning, when the high-pitched buzz of the Emergency Broadcasting System blared over the P.A., we all knew just what to do. We hit the floor, crawled under our desks, and folded our arms over our heads. Nobody laughed. I squeezed my eyes shut and imagined a blinding flash and the whole school blown to smithereens, and then all the kids and teachers would be left out in the open, ducked and covered.

That didn't happen though, at least not that morning. An announcer came on the P.A. and said, "This is only a test. If this had been an actual emergency, you would have been instructed where to go for shelter." I thought about the little igloo in Randy's backyard. If I knocked politely during an air raid, would Mrs. Greene let me in?

At lunch the Official Ritchie Valens Fan Club was supposed to meet at our usual table in the cafeteria, but only me and Mary Lou showed up. We wolfed down our brown bag sandwiches, then spent the rest of the time trying to recruit members. It was tough, especially facing up to the look I got just before a kid said no. Each time I got "the look" it was harder to ask the next person. Five minutes before the bell, Mary Lou had gotten three new members, and I had snagged only four—all girls except Randy. I didn't have the nerve to ask other boys, and I was sorry I asked Randy. A fan club seemed like something only girls would want to be in.

Across the cafeteria, we spotted Brenda eating with Carla Mann and Peggy Jo Peterson. I bumped Mary Lou with my elbow and pointed my chin at her. "Hey, how come we're doing all the work?"

We went over to Brenda as she stood to leave. Her neck was arched far back to look at a very tall boy who had just tapped her shoulder. Not just any boy—Clarence Long, a senior and varsity basketball player. He had a big Adam's apple and bad skin, but he was super popular.

"Did ya forget our meeting?" I asked Brenda.

Clarence looked down at me and muttered, "Beat it, skag."

I felt the heat of a blush rise to my face, but I stood my ground.

"Hey, doll," Clarence said to Brenda, "you sure improve the view of this crummy cafeteria. Why don't ya meet me outside the gym after school?"

She tried to look cool, but I could tell by the way she shook her hair and made it ripple down her back that she was impressed Clarence was speaking to her. She placed her hand on her hip, and said, "What's in it for me?"

I had to admire Brenda's quick thinking. If Clarence talked to me—which he wouldn't—I'd be too tongue-tied to respond.

"I'll buy you a shake at the drive-in, doll face. Strawberry. I bet you like strawberry."

Brenda liked chocolate. She inspected her fingernails. They were stubby and painted red, except she had picked some of the polish off. "I'll think about it."

We waited until Clarence ambled off, then Mary Lou gasped. "You're not really going to meet him, are you, Brenda? I hear he's a wolf."

"That's not the problem." Brenda puffed air into her bangs. "He sweats too much!"

"Jeepers, Brenda, if you play, you gotta sweat," said Mary Lou.

"I don't have to," said Brenda. "I'm glad I'm not a boy."

Mary Lou started blinking real hard. I knew she had wanted to try out for the volleyball team, but she couldn't get up the nerve. Girls who played sports got called sweat hags.

"We got seven new members," I told Brenda. "How many did you get?"

"I'm not wasting my breath recruiting. When we take out our ad in *Sixteen,* we'll get thousands."

I shook my head. "No can do, Brenda. My dad says an ad would cost a lot of money."

"Oh, really?"

"Yeah, really. And he said we don't hafta vote for officers. He said it's my club so I get to be president if I want."

"Your dad *would* say that."

I leaned into her, my arms crossed. "What do you mean by that, Brenda Gardner?"

"You *know*."

Mary Lou and I watched her walk off.

"I don't think your dad is a communist," said Mary Lou.

"Gee, thanks. And I don't think there's anything wrong with sweating."

"My mom says, 'Horses sweat, men perspire, and women glow.'"

"Yeah? Well, then you should glow if you want."

"Lookee!" Mary Lou pointed her chin across the cafeteria where Clarence Long was swinging his lanky arm around Brenda's shoulders. "My dad would kill me if I dated a senior. No, he'd kill the senior. I wonder what Benda's parents would think about it."

"Mrs. Gardner would let her. Anything to be popular."

"Donna!"

"The truth hurts. Since when did Brenda get so stuck up?"

"She's our friend!"

I was beginning to wonder.

After school, when I walked through the garage toward the back door, I saw that the car was gone. With no one home, I had a chance to do a little snooping around. I dug through the stack of old newspapers and found Friday's *San Francisco Chronicle*, *Berkeley Gazette*, and the university's paper, *The Daily Californian*. On the kitchen table, I found that morning's *Chronicle*.

I climbed the stairs, pushed open my door, and was startled to find Alice sprawled on her bed. She quickly stuffed something under her pillow, and I put the newspapers behind my back.

"What are you hiding?" I asked. "Cigarettes?"

Alice sprang off her bed, sauntered over to the desk we shared, pulled cigarettes and matches out of the top drawer, and lit up. "Why would I hide my cigarettes?"

"Because Mom and Dad don't like you smoking."

She inhaled and coughed, waving the smoke away from her face. I turned away so she wouldn't see my grin. It looked cool to smoke only if you were a cool smoker. "They know I smoke. It's one of the many little charades that goes on around here. You don't have to hide those papers, by the way."

"Oh." I set the newspapers on my bed. "Mom told me not to read them. She said the things they said about Dad might upset me."

"Do you do everything the keepers tell you, baby sister?"

"My name is Donna!" I snapped, knowing Alice's usual comeback.

"I'll try to remember that, baby sister."

The "baby sister" stuff had started soon after Alice had begun college that fall. When I complained to Mom, she said, "When kids go off to college for their first term, they suddenly know more than everybody else."

Alice used to be nicer. She used to be a big sister I could look up to. When we were little, Grandma bought us matching Ivory Sweetheart dolls, which now sat on our upper bookshelf. Mine was the one with chocolate stains on the dress, hair sticking out, and one eye that wouldn't stay open, while Alice's doll looked as new as the day we got them. When Alice made her bed, it was smooth and tight while mine was lumpy. When I woke up from a nightmare scared of the dark, she used to turn on the light for me; now half the night she wasn't here at all.

"What are you doing home?" I asked.

"I live here. Unfortunately." When she had been accepted to Cal, she wanted to live in the dorms with the out-of-towners, but Dad said it would be a waste of money. "It's my only chance to be out on my own before I get married," Alice had argued. Our parents fought with her about other things, too. Mom wanted her to major in English, but Alice chose anthropology, whatever that was. "Anything to be different," Mom had said.

I hung up my school dress and changed into pedal pushers. Alice decided she could trust me with what she had slipped under her pillow. It was only a stenographer's notebook. I would have thought nothing of it, but since she had hidden it, I figured it would be worth snooping into when I got the chance.

I lay on the rug and opened Friday's *Chronicle*. It said that John R. Lechner, an executive director of the Americanism Educational League of

Los Angeles, claimed that Leopold K. Kronenberger, a professor of physics at the University of California, "had launched a deliberate and vicious propaganda scheme to implant a universally accepted Communist party line into the minds of our boys and girls."

My scalp prickled to see Dad's name in print linked to such an awful lie. "What's the Americanism Educational League?" I asked Alice.

"It's like a bunch of cubes putting on debates and essay contests to teach us boys and girls how to grow up to be good Americans."

"What else would we grow up to be?"

"Beats me. Reds?"

"Did you write an essay for them when you were applying for scholarships?"

"Those shucksters? My opinions would hit their wastebasket like greased lightning."

"Mrs. Lupine says your opinion doesn't matter in an essay. It's how well you support your opinion that counts."

"Bully for Mrs. Lupine. Look, there's Hitler's Youth, and there's Americanism's Youth. You dig?"

"No." I read some more. An unnamed student said, "Professor Kronenberger told his students that the FBI was a national police organization which operates secretly without public criticism and is therefore a threat to democracy." Dad was quoted next. "I posed it as a question, not as a statement. It's a timely topic—the role of the FBI— and I addressed it for shock value to stimulate a thoughtful response." It was reported that Mr. Lechner wrote a letter to Governor Edmund G. "Pat" Brown charging "Communist propaganda was endorsed in a physics course at the University of California."

The article in Monday's paper was much shorter and said what Randy had told me: Governor Brown had referred the problem to the University of California Board of Regents. It would begin an inquiry into the matter at its January meeting to be held in Riverside. It was November now, and January seemed a long way off.

"Alice, what can the Board of Regents do to Dad?"

She seemed too busy writing in her notebook to answer. Finally she said, "Fire his ass."

It made me blush to think of our own father's behind. I gathered up the papers, went downstairs, and put them back where I had found them.

When I returned to the bedroom, Alice was sitting at the desk again, smoking another cigarette and rifling through my Official Ritchie Valens Fan Club cigar box. "You little sneak, you swiped my index cards."

"Only a few."

"I need them all for my term paper. Oh, what have we here?" Alice extracted a sheet of Mom's perfumed lavender stationery.

"Give it!"

I lunged for the paper, but Alice leaped out of my reach, dramatically reading, "Mrs. Ritchie Valens, Mrs. Ritchie Valens, Mrs. Ritchie Valens." She laughed. "You're getting hitched to a Mexican? Would that ever rattle Mother's cage!"

"He's not Mexican!"

"He sings in Spanish. Where do you think he comes from—Spain?"

"He lives in Los Angeles."

"I'll stick by you, baby sister. You could have a whole caboodle of little brown ankle-biters. I'm hep."

I swan dived across Alice's bed and grabbed her notebook. I was surprised to see she had been writing poetry. At the bottom of a page of scratched out words, she had copied a few clean lines. I read them aloud, mimicking Alice, "Blood iron / gushing down my open thighs filling / my boots weighted / trudging my weary red-soaked existence."

Alice screamed. She snatched the notebook from me and used it to beat me over the head. I giggled and shouted, "Icky!"

"It's not about what you think, you dumb cluck. It's about how women are—oh, you ignorant germ!" Alice tore the poem from the notebook, ripped it into shreds, and flung them into the wastebasket.

"You didn't have to do that," I said quietly. I felt just awful. I wish I hadn't made fun of her poem.

"How can I expect you—how can I expect anyone in this goddamn house to understand me?" she yelled, and because she said "understand" instead of "dig" I knew not even an apology would make it better.

The telephone rang in the hall, and I went to answer it. Dad had coached me on answering crank calls. He said to ask, "Who is speaking?" and that would cause the coward to hang up.

"Hello?" I said.

"Hey, beat chick baby."

I paused. "Who is speaking?"

"Why this is Kenneth, your dreamboat lover boy."

"Do you wanna talk to Alice?"

"Aren't I talking to her now?"

"This is Donna."

When Alice heard her name, she came running. She wrenched the receiver from my grip, and her snarl melted into a coy little smile. "Hey, Big Daddy-o," she said as cool as ice cream. "I told you not to call me here."

I stared at Alice's arched back and one jutted hip. *Daddy-o?* Old people said Daddy-o. Not as old as our parents, but the beatniks who wore all black and hung around the coffee houses on Telegraph Avenue. Why would Alice be interested in one of them when she could date a cute college boy with a letterman sweater and a crew cut?

I shuffled back to our room, sat on my bed, and set the latest *Sixteen* on my lap. In it was a fab article about Ritchie. I opened to his picture and gazed at my dreamboat. I loved his dimple and the black curl that dangled over his forehead, but really, he wasn't that good-looking. It was the way I felt when I played his records that made him the living end. He would never say, "Beat it, skag," to me or any girl. I knew I wasn't ugly, but boys like Clarence Long wanted to make me feel that way. Not my Ritchie. He was real sweet, I could just tell. I lifted the magazine to my face, closed my eyes, and kissed his lips.

CHAPTER THREE

The Shaggy Dog was coming out in January, and Mary Lou, Brenda, and I were dying to see it. It starred two of our favorite Disney actors, Tommy Kirk and Annette Funicello. *Sixteen* claimed it was hilarious, with Tommy turning into a big sheepdog. The plan was that my mom would take Brenda, Mary Lou, and me to the Friday night showing, and my friends would get to sleep over. That day after school, I dashed home to find Mom in bed. It was a bad sign.

When I pushed her bedroom door open, she sat up with an alarmed expression. "Home already, sweetie? My, look at the time! I've got to get up!" She slumped back on her pillows.

"Are you sick?" I knew she wasn't.

"Just a little tired."

Sometimes she called it "tired." Sometimes she called it "nervous." Over the years, Mom stayed in bed whole days, sometimes several. "Will you still be able to take us to the movies tonight?"

She ran her fingers through her mussed hair. "What movie?" Another bad sign.

"Mom! *The Shaggy Dog*! You still have a couple more hours to rest. Do you want me to get you anything? A cup of coffee? Your pink bed jacket?"

"No, thank you, Donna. I'm getting up!" She swung her legs over the side of the bed, but then hunched forward, as if that's all the energy she had. "Don't tell Daddy."

When she stayed in bed all day, my father's smile got extra bright. He bought her a bouquet of flowers, a box of chocolates, or a new bed jacket.

Why would anyone need a jacket to go to bed? Mom had at least a half dozen.

The phone rang, and I went into the hall to answer it.

"I can't go." The voice sounded too deep to be Mary Lou's, but I knew that's who it was. She'd been sneezing and coughing in school all day. "My mom's afraid you and Brenda will catch my cold."

"Oh, pooh. Who cares? This is *The Shaggy Dog!*"

"Can't help it, Don. No can do."

We talked a little longer, and by the time I got off the phone, Mom was up and dressed, and down in the kitchen starting dinner.

"That was Mary Lou. She has a cold, and her mom won't let her come."

"Oh, too bad, Donna. Will you make the carrot and raisin salad?"

While I was peeling carrots, Brenda called.

"I'm sorry to cancel at the last minute, but I won't be able to attend the movie and sleepover tonight," she said, trying to sound like an adult speaking to another adult.

"You can, too," I blurted hotly. "You're just saying you can't because Mary Lou can't."

"That's not true, Donna. I've been looking forward to the movie as much as you, but my mom won't let me go."

"Why not?"

"Because she won't."

"Liar, liar, pants on fire!" I slammed the receiver down and returned to the kitchen. "Brenda isn't coming, either." As I picked up another carrot, a tear rolled down my nose.

"Never mind, sweetie." Mom kissed the top of my head. "We'll go together and enjoy ourselves. What shall we get—Raisinets or Bon Bons?"

"I don't care." Not even a treat from the theater snack bar could cheer me up.

During dinner, Mom cut one of her fish sticks into four neat squares and pushed around her peas with her fork. She never had a big appetite, but since Dad had been accused of spreading Communist propaganda in his classes, she seemed to stop eating entirely. My parents didn't talk about the pending verdict of the University of California Board of Regents around me, but it had loomed over our Christmas and New Year's like a dark cloud. We only had a week more to wait for the Regents' decision.

Dad touched Mom's arm. "Not feeling well, Shirley?"

She pushed her lips into a small, weak smile. "I'm fine, dear. Just a little tired."

"Alice can take Donna to the movies."

My sister dropped her fork with a clatter. "No, Alice can't! Like I'm not going to some drippy kid's movie. Dig?"

Dad raised his thick eyebrows at her. "Alice is gone like day and night. Alice can spend one evening with her sister. Dig?"

I laughed. It was funny to hear Dad mimic Alice's beatnik slang in his German accent.

"Really, Leo, I'm fine," said Mom. "Donna and I will go."

"You rest up, darling." Dad patted Mom's hand. "I'll just drop the girls at the theater and pick them up later."

"Oh, hell, no!" exclaimed Alice. "At least I get the car."

"Not at night."

Alice leaned into Dad. "I can wreck it in the day just as well!"

"Forget it!" I exclaimed. *The Shaggy Dog* wasn't worth my family fighting over it. "I don't want to go!"

Dad held up his broad palm like a stop sign. He reached into his pocket and set the car keys and a five-dollar bill on the table.

With a grin, Alice snatched them up. "Gee, thanks, Daddy. You're the mostest. Come on, baby sister. Let's make the scene!"

I should have been suspicious of Alice's sudden, cheerful cooperation, but she didn't get the car often. We only had one, a 1955 two-tone Oldsmobile sedan, white on top and sky blue on the bottom. Our parents had not allowed Alice to drive until she was a senior, and she hadn't had much practice. She hugged the curb so that I thought we'd climb onto the sidewalk. At one yellow light, she floored the gas pedal, and I clung to the door handle for dear life.

In front of the California Theater on Kittredge, she screeched to a stop in the middle of the street. "Get out," she ordered.

"What?"

"You heard me. I'll pick you up the minute the movie ends, scout's honor."
I stared into the brightly lit, red-and-yellow theater lobby with the sparkling chrome and glass snack bar. I didn't have the nerve to walk in there alone

and sit in the dark by myself. Kids from my school might catch me looking like a loner with no friends.

A horn tooted behind us.

"Cripes," yelled Alice, "get the hell out of the car!"

"No!" I crossed my arms and heaved them onto my chest.

Alice stomped on the gas and off we went with a lurch. "Look, I'm meeting someone at Kip's. Now, Donna, please. I'm going around the block. When we get in front of the theater again, bail out!"

"Drop me off at home, selfish!"

"You're the selfish one. If we go home, Dad won't let me leave again with the car." Alice veered around the corner and headed toward Telegraph Avenue. She was no good at parallel parking and had to turn down a dark narrow street to find a spot she could nosedive into. She looked over my jumper and saddle shoes. "You're a fright! Keep your coat on."

"I'll wait here."

"Suit yourself." Alice wriggled out of the car in her tight, black pedal pushers. I let her go three steps before I realized she really was going to leave me alone in the cold and dark.

I dashed after her. "You used to be nicer."

"I used to be square."

"Can't you be nice and…um…round?"

"Round?"

I had to laugh along with her. Alice was about as round as a toothpick.

Kip's Coffee House was crowded, noisy, and smoky. A large group of college kids had pushed together two of the little round tables. A boy scraped over two more chairs for us to squeeze in.

"We didn't think you'd ever get here, Alice," said one of the girls.

"I got held up." She pointed at me with the top of her head. "Baby sister in tow."

"Hello, baby sister!" some of the kids greeted me.

Alice's friend Darlene scooted close to her. She had black eyeliner all around her eyes that made her look like a raccoon. "Are you meeting Kenneth?"

Alice glanced around the room beneath half-lowered lids. "I never know about him." She fished her cigarettes out of her big handbag and lit up. When the waiter came by she ordered coffee for both of us, knowing I didn't drink coffee, and paid with Dad's five dollars.

Open mike was going on, and anyone who felt the urge could go to the front of the room and perform. Some boys read poetry while others played jazz or folk music. Alice slipped out her stenographer's notebook and flipped through it, pausing to read here and there.

Darlene touched her arm. "You're not really thinking of going up there, Alice! You know what they say about girls writing poetry—women's work."

Alice flashed her brightest, red smile. "Oh, I know! These are Kenneth's poems. He asked me to read a few."

I realized then that there had been only one girl performer, a thin blonde who sang a dozen verses in a soft, high-pitched whine about an annoying person named Barbara Allen who had to go to her grave just because her sweet William did.

The next performer was a saxophonist who played such long, high-pitched wailing sounds that the music was hard to follow, but then he settled into a tune with a swinging beat. Alice and most of her group got up to dance. I was left alone with a boy who wore a black-and-white striped shirt and had a greasy ducktail. He tapped the beat on the tabletop. "Isn't this a gas, baby sister?"

"My name is *Donna*."

"I dig, like Ritchie Valens's Donna?"

How did he know? Could word of the Official Ritchie Valens Fan Club have reached the college set? I pushed back my scarf and tilted my chin. "Why, yes I am."

He tossed his head back in a laugh. "Ritchie's *real* Donna, from Granada Hills? Like his high school sweetheart he wrote the song for?"

The room seemed to shift. I stared at the dancers, not really seeing them. All these months I had been imagining Ritchie singing to me, when in fact it was *another* Donna, a *real* Donna that he held hands with and hugged and maybe even kissed. The lyrics played in my head. "I *had* a girl." Maybe they had broken up! Now Ritchie could forget about that Donna and move on to me, his new Donna! But this reasoning didn't help the sinking feeling in my heart.

Alice and her friends who had been dancing returned to our table. She glanced at her watch, then looked toward the entrance expectantly. The door opened. A tall, muscular man sauntered in, causing Alice's tongue to curl around her upper teeth. He wore dark glasses and a small pointy beard and was carrying bongo drums. He was no college kid. Two firm hands grasping his bare bicep belonged to a sophisticated-looking blond lady in a full white skirt. She was no college kid either. Alice lowered her eyes and her chin went bumpy.

Darlene patted her arm. "Tough luck, kid."

"Ah, I know about *her*. I'm cool with it," said Alice's mouth, but her face didn't agree.

There was no more seating in the packed room so the blond lady had to lean against the wall as Kenneth strode to the stage. The crowd clapped while Alice blew smoke to the ceiling like she wasn't the least bit interested. Kenneth pulled some pages out of his leather bomber jacket and set them on the podium, then perched on a bar stool, grasping the bongos between his knees. He tapped on the drums and lolled his head around, then paused to read a few lines of poetry. It was strange stuff about the Sphinx and Buddha and the H-bomb. He drummed more and read more. Sometimes he slapped the bongos for punctuation, and this made the crowd hoot and shout encouragement. At the end of his performance, his chin bobbed up and down in a cool gesture.

"That cat is hep," said the boy with the ducktail. "He's got like crazy illuminations."

"He's magnificent," Darlene gushed to Alice.

"It wasn't dreadful," Alice said glibly. "Some of the imagery was a little vague."

"Are you wacko?" asked Ducktail. "It was like clashing harmonies, dig?"

"Right-o." Alice flung her notebook into her handbag.

I leaned over the table and shouted to be heard. "Why is he wearing sunglasses? It's *night*."

Ducktail got a kick out of that. "Maybe he's blind."

Alice glared at me like I was a germ. "Keep you voice down, Donna."

A jazz trio started its set with a long drum solo. Alice leaped from her chair and began to dance without a partner, galloping all over the room with jerky movements of her arms and legs, bumping into other dancers.

She pounced on a tabletop, drew her knees up and spun around on her bottom. She jumped off, kicked up her heels, and fell into two boys who began tossing her back and forth until she shoved one of them into a crowded table.

"What's she on?" Ducktail asked in amazement.

"Alice on Alice," said Darlene.

How could this angular, rude dance erupt from the big sister I had looked up to all my life? Our parents would be mortified.

Abruptly, Alice yanked my arm. "Come on, baby sister, let's beat this roach pad."

As we exited, Kenneth slid his dark glasses down his nose and reached out to catch her shoulder, but she brushed him off. As she passed the blond woman, she swung her hip high and bashed it into her backside, causing her to stumble forward.

Out on the sidewalk, I asked, "Is that the Kenneth who called you?"

"You never heard his name, dig?"

"Gosh, Alice, he's a *man* and he was with a *lady*. They're grownups!"

"I'm grown up," said Alice.

"Oh, real grown up. You just butted that lady halfway across the room."

"I did, didn't I?" Alice arched her eyebrows like she was proud of herself. "I know where we can go for some real kicks."

"We're getting hot fudge sundaes?" I asked hopefully.

"Good one, baby sister."

When we got into the car, she turned onto University Avenue, heading toward the Bay Bridge.

"You can't *drive* to San Francisco!"

"How else are we gonna get there—swim?"

With her driving, we probably would have to swim…or sink. I pressed my fingers to my face. "Oh God, we're gonna die."

Alice laughed in a scary way.

On the San Francisco side of the bay, we wove through the traffic on Fisherman's Wharf and headed into North Beach, Coit Tower looming over us like a beacon in the night. We got stuck in a holding pattern, cruising the triangle of Montgomery, Columbus, Broadway, Montgomery, Columbus, Broadway. Alice rolled down her window and craned her neck to peer at the passing nightclubs, galleries, coffee houses, and apartment buildings as the driver in the car behind her rolled down his window and shouted at her, "Drive it or park it."

Alice gripped the steering wheel tighter, leaned forward, and peered out the windshield at various angles.

"Do you even know where you're going?" I asked.

"Sort of. I know it's here somewheres."

We drove by the Purple Onion, the Fox Theater, the Hungry I, then Nam Yuen, Sun Hung Heung, and Sam Wo. "We're gonna eat Chinese food?" I asked.

"Oops." Alice turned sharply and around North Beach we cruised again. "Ah, here it is!"

We found a length of curb she could maneuver into. She clasped my arm as we pushed through the pedestrian traffic. Everyone in the neighborhood seemed to be out roaming the streets in the cold night air. There were beatniks, old men, Oriental people, and wide-eyed tourists, but nobody as young as me. I noticed two things I'd never seen before: a Negro man arm-in-arm with a white lady and two men holding hands, one wearing mascara and eyeliner. Where was Alice taking me—a blaring jazz club, a greasy spoon, a grungy beatnik's pad?

She halted and peered up, her face glowing in a large, brightly lit marque: City Lights Bookstore.

"A bookstore? We're going to a *bookstore*?"

"I hope we're not too late."

"Too late for what?"

Alice slipped by the racks of used books on the sidewalk and joined the crowd heading into the store. I followed her past shelves of paperbacks, newspapers, and magazines, through the door at the back of the triangular building, and down a stairwell. At the entrance of the basement was a tall sign reading, "I am the door." Some of the bookracks had been pushed aside and folding chairs were set up. The narrow room, lit by candlelight, was nearly filled, but by stumbling over a row of people, Alice and I were able to find seats. A hush fell over the audience as a young man with large, black-framed glasses and wild, curly hair approached the podium.

His name was Allen Ginsberg, and he was there to read his poem "Howl." It began with "I saw the best minds of my generation destroyed by madness." He seemed nearly mad himself. His tone was intense, and sometimes he looked up from the page with penetrating eyes, jabbing the air with his forefinger. The bizarre images he conjured were so swift and dense I couldn't follow them. Some of the words didn't seem to go together like "unshaven rooms" and "hydrogen jukebox" and others were so dirty I blushed and stared at my lap. The listeners shouted in agreement or laughed unexpectedly. It was a very long poem. Ginsberg read for over half an hour.

Out on the bustling street again, Alice loped along with outstretched arms and arched neck, intoxicated not on drink, but words.

I ran after her, shouting, "Alice, slow down. Stop acting so crazy."

She turned to grasp my arm. "What did you think, Donna?"

"Uh…I don't think I got it." I shaped my hand into a claw and made circular motions before my stomach. "It made me feel all icky inside."

"That's it!" Alice shouted ecstatically. "That's poetry! If only I could write like Ginsberg! Oh!"

"You would want to? With all those bad words?"

"There are no bad words; there are no good words. Words are not the H-bomb. But what Ginsberg did was so *brave*. How I wish I were that brave!"

I was glad she wasn't. If Alice ever wrote a poem like "Howl," our whole family would die of embarrassment.

It was past eleven by the time we got home. I slipped into my pajamas and got into bed with my new *Sixteen*. I turned to the Ritchie Valens article I'd been saving, and there was the whole story in plain black-and-white. More painful was a photograph of the other Donna, the *real* Donna, sporting a blond bouffant and a radiant smile. Ritchie had been "close" to her for two and a half years. They had met at a garage party where he was playing, long before he got famous. "It was love at first sight," the real Donna was quoted. "He's the sweetest, kindest boy I know."

I let the magazine slip to the floor, feeling the sinking down feeling in my heart for the second time that night. So it was true: Ritchie had a Donna, and she wasn't me.

From the desk came the sound of rustling paper. Alice was flipping through her notebook, tearing out pages, balling them up, and throwing them into the wastebasket. She turned off the light, hurled herself into bed, and pulled the blankets over her head.

I listened for her even breathing, then tiptoed from my bed to the wastebasket. I pulled out the wads of paper, smoothed them out, and pressed them between my mattress and springs, just in case she might need them some day.

CHAPTER FOUR

The day of the University of California Board of Regents' meeting came and went, but Dad didn't hear a thing about its outcome. Mom called it "waiting for the other shoe to drop." On the evening of Tuesday, February third, I was sitting in the living room with Mom, when Dad come through the front door, a newspaper tucked under his arm. Mom traded him a martini for his coat and hat, and he kissed her.

"Any news, Leo?"

"There is," Dad said in a neutral tone.

"Oh! Good or dreadful? Don't keep me in suspense another minute!" Mom's voice was muffled as she hung up his things in the hall closet.

Dad made a flourish with his arm as he lifted his drink. He tasted it and smacked his lips. "Ah, perfect, darling. Thank you for taking such good care of me."

Mom laughed. "Leo! What's the verdict?"

"Patience, my dear. Let me take a load off my feet." Dad looked over at me, sprawled on the sofa. "Hello, Donna girl, how was school?"

I shrugged. "Same as usual."

"What did you learn today?"

"Leo, please!" Mom interrupted.

Dad settled in his big chair and read aloud from the *Daily Californian* like he was giving a speech, "'The Regents of the University of California deeply regret that an improper question appeared on a physics quiz that casts reflection on the Federal Bureau of Investigation. Steps are being taken to prevent a recurrence of a similar, unfortunate incident. The university has the highest respect for the FBI as an essential arm of the nation's security and of the rule of law which is the keystone of our democratic society.'" Dad dropped the paper in his lap. "Ha! The bunch of ninnies! Kowtowing to J. Edgar Hoover! Keystone to democracy—nonsense!"

"What steps, Leo? What *steps* are being taken?" Mom asked anxiously. "Has the president of the university called you in?"

Dad swatted the air. "No."

"What about Aldridge? As chairman of the physics department, it must be his duty to chastise you."

"Not a word. Not even passing in the hallway."

Mom crossed her arms. "The silent treatment. This is bad."

"Don't worry, darling, I have tenure."

"What's tenure?" I asked.

"It means the university can't give me the boot." Dad drained his glass and handed it to Mom for a refill, but she didn't budge.

"It's starting again, isn't it, Leo?"

"What's starting again?" I asked, looking from Mom to Dad, trying to read their expressions.

Dad leaned forward, jabbing the air. "The government has nothing on me, Shirley. They went through my background with a fine tooth comb before, and they couldn't find a blessed thing that links us with any communists."

Alice burst through the front door, heaving breathlessly. "I came home as soon as I heard the news! Doesn't that just beat all?" She flung her armload of books in a chair and sank next to me on the sofa. "Oh, Donna, I'm so sorry about Ritchie!"

It took a moment to realize she was talking about Ritchie Valens. I hadn't much thought about him since I discovered there was a real Donna. Now I was busy thinking about the Rosenbergs, Mr. and Mrs. Rosenberg both, sent to the electric chair, leaving their children orphans. "What can they do to you, Daddy?" I asked.

"You're not to worry about this, Donna. Do you understand?"

There was worry in my father's voice. There was worry in my mother's shaking hands. Alice looked crushed, and lately, she didn't seem to care about anything that had to do with us.

I ran up the stairs, threw myself on my bed, and cried into my pillow. Soon I felt Alice stroking my hair. She hadn't done that in ages. I sat up.

"Alice, do you believe Daddy is a communist?"

"Nope."

"Is Dr. Tucker or any of the other professors communists?"

"If they are, they keep a lid on it. It isn't proper to be a Red in polite society these days."

"Beatniks aren't part of polite society. Are beatniks communists?"

Alice raised a shoulder and let it drop. "They usually aren't anything political."

"Are Nazis communists?"

"Hitler hated commies. He fought against them in the war."

"So Dad couldn't be a Nazi *and* a communist at the same time," I reasoned.

"Dad was never a Nazi."

I was certain Alice was wrong about this. "Yes, he was, I mean in the old days. He talks just like Nazis do in movies, and Dr. Tucker always calls him 'you old Nazi.'"

"He's joking! You don't understand any of this."

I clutched her sleeves. "I want to, Alice! Explain it to me, please!"

She blew out a deep breath. "O.K. It's true Dad taught physics at the University of Vienna, but he hated Hitler! When nuclear fission was discovered, Hitler ordered Dad and a bunch of other physicists to work on the atom bomb, but Dad gave the Nazis the slip."

"Dad did too work on the bomb!"

"Not for Hitler, dweeb. For us, the US."

I was quiet a moment, letting it all sink in. "Then why would he get into so much trouble for writing a little question in his physics class about the FBI?"

"Because the government is always keeping an eye on him. He knows a lot of secret science stuff. They're afraid he might sell it to a spy or give it away to the commies."

"He would not!" I said indignantly.

Alice's mouth formed a firm, straight line. "Tell that to J. Edgar Hoover."

She got up, went to the desk, and began doing homework, while I just sat there staring across the room. After a while, I thought to ask, "What were you going to say about Ritchie?"

"Oh! You still don't know." She stuck out her lower lip and shook her head sadly. I braced myself, expecting her to say he had married the real Donna. "He's gone, baby."

"Gone where?"

She lifted her shoulders and let them drop. "His plane crashed."

"*He's dead?*" I slapped my lap. "That's impossible! He's too young to die!"

"Here. See for yourself." Alice handed me the *San Francisco Chronicle*, and I read all about it. Ritchie wasn't the only one. Buddy Holly and the Big Bopper had died, too. They had all played a big concert at the Surf Ballroom, in Clear Lake, Iowa, then boarded a chartered plane a little past midnight. It was stormy weather, and their plane went down in a cornfield only a few miles away. I felt sad, but I wasn't devastated. I guess I fell off Cloud Nine the day I learned there was a real Donna. Now I felt embarrassed by my silly crush on a rock 'n' roll singer, and I hoped everyone would forget the Official Ritchie Valens Fan Club had ever existed.

I turned over on my back and stared up at the ceiling, my thoughts drifting back to Dad. "Alice?"

"Hmm?" She was taking notes on index cards from a bunch of books and magazines strewn around her.

"Would it bother you if I asked another question?"

"Naw, I'm just gathering facts for my Chambri term paper."

"What's that?"

"This female-dominated tribe in New Guinea. The ladies call all the shots. Sounds like the living end."

"Oh. Do *you* know any communists?"

She clicked her ballpoint pen against her chin. "I know of one. This old guy who hangs around Kip's, bumming cups of coffee and reading subversive newspapers."

I sprang up on the heels of my hands and twisted to look at Alice. "Could you introduce me?"

"I don't really know him. I don't want to get started with him. If I talked to him once, he'd never leave me alone, and I go into Kip's all the time. Why don't you talk to him?'

I couldn't believe what Alice was suggesting. "All by myself? I'd be too scared."

"Air Man won't bite. He'll just talk your ear off."

"Air Man? How'd he get such a funny name?"

"Beats me. Maybe 'cause he's full of hot air."

"You're saying I should just walk into Kip's one day after school and start talking to a stranger, just like that?"

"That would be cool, baby sis. Do it, then clue me in."

We both laughed, I'm not sure why. I picked up the newspaper again and gazed at the picture of the little crumpled airplane. "Poor Ritchie."

Talk of Dad's innocent but thought-provoking quiz question refused to go away. For weeks it was a popular topic on the op-ed pages of all the Bay Area newspapers: the *Oakland Tribune,* the *Berkeley Gazette,* the *San Francisco Chronicle* and *Examiner,* and, of course, the *Daily Californian.* Many people wrote in support of Dad:

"In the face of public criticism, the Regents took the easiest, rather than the best, way out."

"We have too many sacred cows in this society. Since when has the FBI become such a hallowed institution that we can no longer freely discuss it?"

"The purpose of a university is to teach its students to intelligently criticize all things—books, plays, philosophy, political thought and even the United States government."

"Using the words 'Communist' or 'leftist' or 'liberal' as a cover-up for everything which is displeasing or embarrassing is the greatest boon to the destruction of American society."

But some of the other letters were against Dad, favoring the Regents:

"We should force the University of California to teach our boys and girls the truth about our great democracy, not lies like that one about the FBI being a police force."

"Our great military commanders and the American Legion should give compulsory courses on Americanism for students and faculty alike."

"That communist professor at Cal should be straightened out with proper discipline and forced to teach our red-blooded American children about freedom, democracy, and the worship of God."

No letter drew as much attention as the one that was reprinted in all the newspapers from J. Edgar Hoover himself:

> I was deeply shocked to learn such an erroneous and misleading question concerning the FBI could appear in a University of California physics test. This question categorically termed the FBI a national police organization. Nothing could be more wrong. The FBI at all times is accountable to the Attorney General and the President. Each year I appear before Committees of the Congress to explain the operation of the FBI. Likewise, as you know, the courts of this country examine FBI investigative procedures in our cases, which come to trial. Moreover, the FBI is constantly under the scrutiny of an alert and intelligent press. Surely, with these facts, to call the FBI a national police is a gross distortion of fact and a slur on our constitutional form of government.

> My associates join me in expressing appreciation for bringing this matter to the attention of your readers. Only by setting forth the truth can error be combated.

> J. Edgar Hoover

Dad got a chuckle out of Hoover's letter. Over meatloaf and mashed potatoes he said, "Notice how old J. Edgar worked in all three branches of government. That's to distract us from the two basic facts about the FBI: it is a police organization and it is national."

"I'll bet the FBI is gonna start a file on you," joked Alice.

Dad raised his heavy eyebrows. "They could borrow the one the CIA has, but apparently the two organizations never share information. Ha! They think it's a competition!"

"What does CIA stand for?" I asked.

"Never mind, Donna," said Mom. "Clear the table. Now, who wants Jell-O?"

Brenda invited Mary Lou and me over to her house after school, along with several other girls in our class. The Gardners' whole basement was a rec room with a ping-pong table, TV, and hi-fi. Brenda said this is where her mom liked her "to entertain."

Mrs. Gardner had on a tiny frilly hostess apron over a party dress no mom would wear just around the house. She served us Cokes in bottles with straws and little cocktail wieners wrapped and baked in biscuits so it seemed more like a planned party rather than an after-school visit.

We were all laughing and talking and watching *American Bandstand* when Brenda abruptly turned off the TV and stood before us like she was about to make a speech. "You're all probably wondering why I invited you here today."

"For fun?" I asked.

"Well, yeah, but besides that. This is actually the first meeting of the Official Ricky Nelson Fan Club."

"He's dreamy," said Carla Mann, rolling her eyes to the ceiling. Actually one eye went up, the other one drifted to the left. Plus her hair was so frizzy no amount of Aqua Net could tame it. She always followed the queen bee of the moment, currently Brenda, in hopes of gaining some popularity herself.

While Brenda continued to talk up her fan club, I picked up a ping-pong paddle and bounced a ball on it. She glared at me. "Do you mind, Donna? I can't hear myself think."

"Oh, sorry," I said, like I obviously wasn't. I gave the ball a few more bounces just to bug her.

"Now, this won't be any cheap club," said Brenda. "In fact it's rather high class. It's gonna cost you two dollars in dues, but I guarantee it will be worth every penny in quality products. Now, who's in?"

Peggy Jo Peterson raised her hand like she was in school. "Me!"

"Me!"

"Me, too!"

"Two dollars?" I said. "I don't like Ricky Nelson *that* much."

"You're just jealous cuz Ricky sings to Mary Lou instead of you," said Brenda.

Mary Lou flushed a proud pink. "Oh, no. It's just that Donna's loss is probably still fresh in her broken heart."

I had to think what loss she meant, even though Ritchie Valens had been dead only a week. "I don't want to be in anybody's fan club. The whole thing is kinda for babies."

My friends looked at me solemnly. I noticed a few blushes. It grew very quiet. I hadn't meant to insult anybody, not even Brenda.

She shook back her hair so that it rippled to her waist. "Well! You didn't think it was for babies when you were in charge."

I couldn't think of any comeback, so I stood. "I gotta go." I didn't want to leave, not really. I wanted to stay with my friends and swoon over rock 'n' roll idols and pour over hairstyles in magazines and gossip about necking parties. I wanted to care as much about all that stuff as they did, but some unexplainable urge was pushing me up Brenda's basement stairs.

Outside on the sidewalk, my feet weren't taking me in the direction of my house. I wandered across the university campus and through Sather Gate onto Telegraph Avenue. As I strolled past Kip's Coffee House, I spotted an old man at the window, reading a newspaper and basking in the weak February sunlight. A few steps further, I turned around and passed him again. I steered my shaking legs into Kip's and stood before the man, waiting for him to notice me. He had no hair on the top of his head, but the sides and back were white and long, pulled back in a rubber band. His forehead had a lot of purple spots on it, and his beard, lying on his chest, was flecked with crumbs and tobacco juice. He was so gross, I almost lost my nerve. He looked up from his *Daily Worker* with a start.

"Are you Air Man?" I blurted.

He squinted at me. "Who wants to know?"

"Just me. I'm Donna."

"If you're selling anything, I don't have any money."

"I'm not selling anything. I...would you like some coffee?"

"Are you buying, sister?"

I went to the counter and bought a cup of coffee for Air Man and a donut for myself. When I returned to his table and set the coffee before him, he asked, "Where's my donut?"

I went back and got him one, then settled across from him at his table. "May I ask you a question?"

"I'm not sure." He squinted at me. "You wearing a wire?"

"Huh?"

He wiped the corners of his mouth, suppressing a smile. "Shoot."

"Well, I hope you don't think I'm being too forward, but are you a communist?"

"Are you the FBI?"

"No!"

"HUAC?"

"What's Hew-ack?"

"House of Un-American Activities Committee."

I laughed. It sounded like a joke.

"Yeah, I'm a commie."

"Are you a commie pinko or just a regular commie?"

"Plain vanilla. What's it to ya, sister?"

"I used to think all communists lived in Russia. How come you're one?"

"I joined the party when I joined the Wobblies, back in the thirties."

"Wobblies? What a funny name."

"Short for Industrial Workers of the World, a labor union. We fought for a fair wage for a fair day's work."

"That doesn't sound so bad."

"It's not. It's good." He dunked his donut in his coffee, took a bite, and smacked his lips.

"So why does everyone hate communists?"

"Senator Joe McCarthy claimed communists were trying to overthrow the government and force us to be part of the Soviet Union."

I looked around to make sure no one was listening and leaned into him. "Are you trying to overthrow the government?"

He waved his hand. "Naw, I'm a man of ideas, not action, a *luftmensch*. That's Yiddish. It means Air Man."

"Oh. Why would Americans want to give up their freedom and join Russia?"

"No one I know would. You know about the Red Scare, don't you, sister?"

I shook my head.

"Old Joe McCarthy and his friends, Nixon and them, wanted power so they scared folks into thinking communists had infiltrated the government.

Here, dip." He pushed his coffee over to me. It had crumbs from his donut in it and probably his germs, too. He nodded his head and said, "Try it. It's good that way."

Hesitantly, I dunked my donut and bit into it. It wasn't bad. "Why would people believe McCarthy?"

"Because they're afraid. 'An age without fear is an age without hope.' Don't remember who said that."

It didn't make any sense to me, but I continued on. "I'm trying to figure out what all of this has to do with my dad."

"Who's your dad?"

"Leopold Kronenberger."

Air Man whistled. "Oh, he's famous."

"Yeah, just for writing a little quiz question."

"What? I'm talking about when he sided with Oppie against the Super. Took the fall with Oppie, he did."

I knew he was talking about Robert Oppenheimer, but I didn't know what he meant about "the fall." I shook my head. "You lost me."

"Your dad worked for Lawrence Livermore Lab after the war, know that?"

"Yes, and then he decided to go back into teaching."

Air Man shook his head. "He decided nothing, sister. He was removed as a security risk."

I stared back at Air Man. I had no proof that he knew what he was talking about, and yet it was sort of what Alice had been trying to explain to me. "That's not fair!"

Air Man nodded. "Lots and lots of people took the fall, sister. McCarthy just had to point his finger at a fella and—*bang!*—his life was ruined. There's scientists, professors, writers who will never work again. Blacklisted by McCarthy."

"Do you think McCarthy will try to get my dad in trouble now?"

"Old Joe can't touch your pop. He's been dead a couple of years. Drank himself to death, he did." Air Man pushed his coffee toward me. "Here, sister, dip."

CHAPTER FIVE

When I answered the door, I heard the *Dragnet* theme playing in my head: Dun-da-dun-dun. *Dun*! The FBI agents standing on our porch wore trench coats and fedoras and flashed their badges just like Sergeant Friday and his partner, but they didn't act like TV stars. One looked sleepy and needed to shave; the other one seemed bored.

"What's your name, little girl?" asked the bored one in a monotone.

"Miss Donna Kronenberger." I made a slight curtsey.

Dad clasped my shoulders from behind and nudged me aside. "These gentlemen are here to see me, not you."

The sleepy G-man opened his eyes a little wider. "Dr. Kronenberger, we'd like to ask you a few questions."

"That's what Sergeant Friday says!" I opened the door wider for them to come in. Mom took their hats and coats.

"Who's Sergeant Friday?" asked Monotone. "Local police?"

I laughed so hard he narrowed his eyes at me. I wondered what it would take to get him to crack a smile.

"She's talking about something on TV, Grayson," said his partner.

Mom offered the FBI agents coffee and bowls of ice cream, and I served them. It was right before dinner, and we never ate ice cream then. That was cocktail hour.

"This is delicious!" Sleepy was wide-awake now, pleased with the refreshments. "Now, I know it's not vanilla."

"It's lemon," I said, getting settled in the armchair in the corner of the room that nobody ever used.

"Donna, don't you have homework to do?" Mom asked.

"Nope."

She hooked an eyebrow in my direction. "Donna, you are excused."

"I won't interrupt, I promise."

"Donna," warned Dad.

"O.K.," I muttered dejectedly. I trudged up the stairs and firmly closed my bedroom door, then tiptoed back to sit on the top step.

One question Dad had to answer was "Are you now or have you ever been a member of the Communist party?"

"No," he responded simply.

"Do you know any members of the Communist party?"

"Several."

"What are their names?"

"I won't name names."

"Why would you withhold information from the United States government?"

"To protect the constitutional rights of the innocent," said Dad. "To prevent you from barging into their homes and disrupting their personal lives. To ensure you won't rob them of their livelihood by blacklisting them."

"Blacklisting? What do you mean?" asked Monotone.

"You know," Dad said gruffly.

"Why do you lecture against the FBI in your university classes?"

"I never did that. I posed a question: could a national police organization be a danger to democracy? For example, the wiretap the FBI has placed on my telephone. It's illegal. Do you find it as ironic as I do that the FBI behaves like the KGB?"

"Leo!" exclaimed Mom. "I don't believe it's quite like that!"

The federal agents returned several more times throughout the spring and summer. During another session, one agent asked Dad to sign the California Loyalty Oath:

> I do swear that I do not advocate, nor am I a member of any party or organization, political or otherwise, that now advocates the overthrow of the Government of the United States or of the State of California by force or violence or other unlawful means...

My father refused to sign.

As soon as I heard the front door shut, I ran downstairs. "Are they gone?"

"For now," said Dad.

"Did I miss anything?" I asked.

"By sitting on the stairs? I think you'd make a great FBI agent yourself, Donna girl. You're certainly nosey enough."

"Aw, Dad!" We laughed together, but Mom didn't join in.

"Leo, they might go easier on you if you cooperated with them in some small way."

"I am supposed to promise not to overthrow the United States government? What makes them think I would do such a thing? What makes them think I wouldn't do it just because I signed their ridiculous paper?"

"It's just a formality," said Mom.

"That Loyalty Oath is unconstitutional! It's an erosion of our civil rights. The Supreme Court will rule against it in due time." Dad went behind the bar to pour himself a drink. "Want one, Mommy?"

"Just a splash, please, darling."

Dad handed her the drink and settled in his chair with his own. Mom leaned toward him so he could light her cigarette.

"You could be dismissed from the university," she said. "Tenure isn't always a sure thing. I'm thinking of those eight professors and administrators at San Francisco State College who were fired for not signing the Loyalty Oath."

Dad shifted his eyes to me and grinned. "Mommy worries too much." There were yellowish rings under his arms on his white work shirt, and his own drink was much taller than a splash. It was obvious even to me that he was worried, too.

One lazy afternoon in June, I lay on my bed reading while Mom cleaned in Dad's study. She was in there a long time banging things around. I went to see what was going on. She was leaning far into a filing cabinet, and she had stacked a tower of file folders on Dad's desk. Sensing my presence, she straightened up with a start. "Donna, don't sneak up on me like that!"

"I didn't sneak up on anybody. What are you doing with Dad's files?"

"Just a little spring cleaning."

It was well past spring, and I had never seen more than one or two of Dad's folders out at once. I guessed he wasn't going to like a whole pile on his desk, and I was right. When he returned from the university and dropped his briefcase in his study, he shouted down the stairs, "Shirley, what's going on in here?"

"Those are the sensitive ones," she called up. "I meant to put them in the incinerator myself, but then I thought you'd better have a second look at them and do it yourself."

I heard the scraping of a filing cabinet drawer and the shuffling of papers. After a few moments, I crossed the hall toward the bathroom as an excuse to snoop. Through the cracked door of his study, I saw Dad replacing all his folders.

Within the week, the FBI agents arrived at our house with a search warrant and confiscated all of Dad's papers. It was a warm July evening. I was washing the dinner dishes, but I took care not to rattle the pots and pans so loudly that I couldn't hear the conversation in the next room.

The agents asked Dad a lot of questions about his past in Austria. Where was he born? What were the names and birth dates of his parents and brother? They were all dead, Dad said, and then the agents asked the dates of their deaths. How had Dad spent his childhood? What had he studied? Where had he taught? How had he come to the United States? This was information they had gone over a couple of other times, and I wondered why the FBI agents asked Dad the same questions over and over.

Toward the end of the interrogation, one of the agents said, "Dr. Kronenberger, we'll need to take your passport."

"What?" exclaimed Mom. "You're not suggesting Leo would defect? Where ever do you think he'd go?"

"Mrs. Kronenberger, are you aware that your husband is a bigamist?"

There was a long pause. I had to hold perfectly still and strain my ears to hear Mom's faint whisper. "Yes."

I hurriedly washed the skillet, drained the water, and skipped scrubbing the sink. I sprinted upstairs and lunged for the dictionary across Alice, who sat at the desk typing a paper for her summer school class. I looked up the word "bigamist" then sucked in air. "I don't believe it!"

"Now what?"

"Dad is married to Mom and another lady at the same time!"

"Oh, that. I know."

"You do? How can he be? He's always with us."

"You dweeb! He married his first wife a long time ago, back in Austria. I overhead Aunt Lillian and Aunt Irene gossiping about it a couple of years ago at camp. When Dad and Mom were first getting to know each other, he told her he wasn't free to marry, but she said she didn't care about his past and married him anyway."

"Do you think Dad had any kids with the Austrian lady?"

"A son. He was just a baby when Dad left."

"Holy moly." I sank to the edge of my bed. I wanted to feel just the same about my father as I always had, but I couldn't. How could he leave his wife and little baby? "I always thought Dad was by himself when he left Austria."

"No one's really alone, baby sister. If you walked out our front door right this minute, you'd be leaving family and friends behind—a whole life."

"But I'd write letters! I'd come back and visit."

"Not in war. Not if you left your country to go work for the enemy." Alice slapped the desk. "Bloody hell! I forgot to leave room at the bottom of the page for the footnotes. Now I have to retype the whole page." Alice ripped the papers out of the typewriter.

"The G-men took Dad's passport. I guess they're afraid he's going to go visit..." I swallowed hard. "his other family."

"Right-o!" Alice exclaimed in her singsong sarcastic tone, "and then he's going to jump a plane from Vienna to Moscow. Those G-men are a joke."

My next question was ridiculous, but I had to ask it. "Do you think Dad would ever leave us?"

"Never!"

"But what about his other family?"

"Ancient history."

"I'm going to ask him about them."

"Donna, no!"

"Why not?"

"Because bigamy isn't discussed. And if you don't talk about some things, it's like they never happened, dig?"

"That doesn't make any sense."

"Right-o, but that's the way the world works." Alice aligned two fresh pieces of onionskin paper with the carbon paper between them and carefully rolled them into the typewriter. She pushed the carriage to the right and began to type again.

"I'll just say to him—"

"You want to kill him?" Alice leaned over her typewriter and glared at me with bug eyes. "It was war! A lot worse stuff happened to millions of other people."

"I know," I whined. Other people weren't our father, though. "Alice?"

"Stop bugging me! I told Angela I'd be over an hour ago."

"Who's Angela?" I asked innocently.

Alice didn't answer, but I knew. I had picked up a lot of information by listening to her talk on the phone to Darlene and her other friends. Angela was that blond lady who was with the beatnik Kenneth at Kip's, the night Alice dragged me along. Angela and Kenneth lived together without being married, and if that wasn't bad enough, Alice was dating Kenneth, too, and now Angela and Alice were friends. It sounded so icky, I didn't breathe a word of it to anybody, not even Mary Lou. How could Alice stand to be with someone else's boyfriend? For that matter, how could Mommy stand to marry Dad when she knew he already had a wife? Things had gone all topsy-turvy, and I didn't know what to make of it.

"Alice?" I called tentatively. When she ignored me, I said. "We got a brother."

She looked up with a grin. "Right-o."

CHAPTER SIX

I had a lot to think about that summer and not much to do. Dad went off to the university every day, not to teach, but to do his own work. Mom stayed late in bed most days, but she was up and dressed before Dad got home. Brenda and I weren't friends anymore. I got together with Mary Lou sometimes, but we were no longer close. She and Carla Mann were doing most of the work in the Official Ricky Nelson Fan Club and acted like they were best friends. Best friends changed; I already knew that. Still it was lonely when it happened.

I watched a lot of TV: *Father Knows Best, Leave It to Beaver, Ozzie and Harriet, The Donna Reed Show, Make Room for Daddy*. These shows had an American family just like mine, except they were nothing like it. They had problems, but nothing that couldn't be solved in a half hour. Beaver's big brother Wally asked a girl out who was too tall for him, but she wore low heels and a flat hairdo. The *Father Knows Best* family's car broke down on the way to a family reunion potluck, but then they ate the baked beans they had brought and enjoyed each other's company. None of these families had a foreign-born dad who was interrogated by the FBI, a mom who stayed in bed all day, and a wild daughter who ran around with beatniks.

When there was nothing good on TV, I took a walk. At first I just went around and around my block, but eventually I started branching out, up the hill to Codornices Park, where there was a long slide I could speed down if I found the right piece of cardboard; down to Shattuck Avenue to the Thrifty's where they sold nickel ice cream cones; across town to the university, and even beyond the campus where I could peer in the windows of the coffee houses and stores on Telegraph Avenue.

One evening I stayed out too long, until almost dark. I ran all the way home in a panic, certain I'd be grounded. I sprinted up our driveway, and up popped a man out of our bushes. I leaped back, clutching my throat and erupting with an "Ach!" By then I recognized him.

"I didn't mean to rattle your cage," said Kenneth, with a mocking grin. He was wearing all black and his greasy hair was slicked back. He smelled of cigarette smoke, booze, and B.O.

"What are you doing in our bushes?"

"Trying to make the scene with Alice."

"Why don't you just come to the door and ring the bell like a human being?"

I meant it as an insult, but he just thought it was funny. "You must be baby sister."

"I'm Donna."

His glittering dark eyes raked over me in a nasty way. "You're not so bad. From the way Alice talks about you, I thought you'd look like something that came out from under a rock."

"Alice isn't home. She's out on a date with her boyfriend."

"Are you sure about that?"

He knew I was lying, and I couldn't think of a comeback. I tossed my head and started toward the house. His arm snaked around me and yanked me close. He pressed his lips to mine and kissed me roughly, painfully squeezing my tender breast. I had to get away, but I was too shocked to move. I just stood there like a ninny until he let me go.

He leered down at me with black pupils wide as saucers. "Oh, so you like me."

I finally was able to send an impulse from my brain to my legs. I dashed up the porch steps and burst through the door. Canned laughter wafted from the TV. Mom was stitching her embroidery and Dad was reading the paper. Neither of them seemed to notice how late I was. I bounded up the stairs, two at a time. Alice was in our room, seated at the vanity, pursing her mouth as she applied red lipstick. She caught my face in the mirror and turned to me. "What's the matter with you?"

I leaned against the door, gasping for air. I had to say something. "What's the matter with you?"

Alice rolled her eyes. She grabbed her beret and swung one leg over the windowsill.

"Don't go!" I pleaded, but she was already gone from me, from Mom and Dad, clamoring down the trellis without another word.

I paced in circles, rubbing my arms. I felt ashamed, humiliated, dirty. I needed to tell somebody, but who? Not Mom, not Dad, no one I could think of. How could I even utter the words, "A man touched my breast," when I had done nothing to stop him? How would I ever get past this terrible feeling of self-disgust?

I drew a bath so hot that my skin turned flaming pink. In bed I tried to read *Donna Parker*, but all I could see was Kenneth's leering eyes, his lips magnified, his mouth opening like a fish. I hated him, but what good did that do?

Harsh sunlight was streaming into my room by the time I awoke. Alice had gone to her summer school class. I didn't want to get out of bed. My stomach growled, but I didn't even want to go down to the kitchen for a bowl of cereal. I stared up at the ceiling, that awful moment playing over and over in my brain like a movie. He had touched my breast, he had kissed me with his open mouth, I had felt his lumpy, slimy tongue. If you don't talk about things, it's like they never happened.

Bump, bump, bump went Randy's basketball. I pulled myself up, shuffled to the window, and spied on him between the wall and the curtain. In January, he had given up trying to walk me to school, and since then we had hardly spoken to each other. I was glad when he had stopped bugging me, but now I sort of missed him. His ball made a pleasant *whoosh* going through the basket fastened to his garage. He had been shooting baskets all summer and was pretty good, despite his height.

Suddenly I wanted to do something physical. I put on a sleeveless blouse, my dungarees rolled up to mid-calf, and tennis shoes. I walked up Randy's driveway and, without saying a word, started dribbling and hurling the ball toward the basket.

"Are you having a nice summer, Donna?" Randy asked.

"No."

"What have you been up to?"

"Nothing."

"Are you looking forward to school starting?"

"No."

"What classes are you taking?"

"Don't know."

He gave up on conversation then. We just tossed the ball around. It was undignified for a girl my age to be playing outside with a boy, especially a shrimpy dork like Randy. People driving by could see me, maybe some of the kids from school. Maybe it would get back to Brenda, and she'd have a good laugh about it, but I didn't care. Slamming the ball hard on the concrete felt good. I played until sweat trickled down my nape and made my ponytail limp. Not sweat, *glow.*

When we stopped to get a drink out of the hose, Randy asked, "Wanna go watch the telephone booth stuffing?"

"Oh, is that this morning?"

"I think so, yeah."

I hesitated, considering the offer. Seeing how many people could fit in a telephone booth had gained local popularity since March, when *Life* magazine had featured a photograph taken in Moraga, about twelve miles away, of twenty-two St. Mary's College students crammed into one phone booth. Some boys from Berkeley High were determined to go down in history for breaking St. Mary's record. I had never witnessed a stuffing and thought it would be swell, but would I want to be seen there with Randy?

"Is Clarence Long still in charge?" My ears burned at the thought of him calling me skag.

"Far as I know," said Randy.

"He graduated."

Randy shrugged. "A lot of his stuffing team did. So what? They're alumni."

"Let me go change," I said.

"You look fine the way you are."

"Are you kidding?" I felt the grains of dried sweat on my cheek. I ran toward my house.

"Hey, Donna!" Randy called after me. "You're coming back, aren't you?"

"Yeah, sure." I dashed upstairs, washed my face, and put on a sundress. As I brushed my hair, I spied Alice's lipstick lying on the vanity. I pressed it to my lips, making tiny dots of color, and rubbed them in. Gazing into the mirror, I widened my eyes, dipped my chin, and smiled faintly.

When I got back outside, Randy and I walked to Shattuck and University, where the designated stuffing booth stood. Not only were there a bunch of kids from our school, but people on the street had stopped to watch. We found out that several attempts had been made, but twenty boys was the highest number to be stuffed so far.

All the boys were in their stocking feet or barefooted, wearing T-shirts and shorts or trousers. Three boys were curled on the floor of the booth, while other boys were stacked on top, some boys peeking between the legs and elbows of others, and some riding piggyback. Randy walked around the booth, rubbing his chin and taking note of the positions of the boys. Just when it seemed that not another person could fit, Clarence smashed into front center to grin into a newspaper reporter's camera.

"I can't breathe," groaned one of boys at the bottom.

"Damn it! Get your foot out my eye!"

"*Ow! Ow!* Leg cramp!"

In a writhing mass of legs and arms, the boys tumbled out of the booth onto the sidewalk, laughing, panting, groaning, and shrieking.

"Twenty-one fellas!"

"That's it! That's the best we can do!"

"No it isn't," said Clarence. "If St. Mary's can do twenty-two, we can do twenty-three."

"We can't win," said Clarence's friend, Alfred, a graduate who had been starting point guard. "That was our best right there."

"I'm through," said one boy who had been at the bottom.

"Me, too," said another.

"Replacements!" hollered Clarence. "Who's going for the next record attempt?" Several boys stepped forward. "O.K., now, you three fellas take the bottom positions."

One boy took a step back. "Oh, no, I'm not going down there again. I'm too young to die."

"You'll do as the master crammer says or get lost," said Clarence.

"I'm lost," said the boy, walking off.

"Replacement!" Clarence yelled. Randy tapped him on the shoulder. Clarence looked down into his face. "Where'd you come from, drip? Off the bottom of somebody's shoe?"

"If you wanna stuff more guys, they gotta be smaller," said Randy.

Clarence worked his mouth, which seemed to be some indication that he was also working his brain. "O.K., smallest fellas in first. You, you, and you," he ordered, pointing at various participants.

Randy tapped Clarence again. "Not just small boys first. *All* small boys. You and Alfred need to bow out!"

"Who asked you?" Clarence planted both palms on Randy's chest and gave him a shove.

Alfred caught him, preventing Randy from falling off the curb. Randy scurried out of the way as Alfred met Clarence eyeball to eyeball. "He's right, you know, Clar. I'll step aside for the sake of good ole Berkeley High."

"Well, I won't," said Clarence. "This is my stuffing, and I'm gonna be a part of it."

"You gotta make sacrifices for the team," insisted Alfred. "Hold him, men."

Alfred and several other boys held Clarence as he struggled against them. Meanwhile all the small and medium-sized boys packed into the telephone booth. "Nineteen, twenty," the crowd counted together, "twenty-one, twenty-two."

"That's it," someone cried at the bottom of the pile. "You're killing me."

"*Ge-ron-i-moooooooooo!*" Randy whooped. He made a running dash for the booth, and without pausing to take off his hard-soled shoes, climbed hips, shoulders, and faces, in order to squeeze into the very top position.

"Twenty-three!" everyone shouted at once. "We beat St. Mary's!"

The photographer snapped the picture that landed on the front page of that evening's *Berkeley Gazette*, with Randy's head ducked down and twisted toward the camera, his glasses dangling from one earpiece and Clarence in the background, grimacing as he struggled against his captors.

Randy treated me to a maple nut nickel cone at Thrifty's, and as we walked up Cedar Street toward home, I was grinning to myself, the telephone booth stuffing playing like a movie in my mind.

"Wanna go see *Plan Nine*?" Randy asked.

"I don't know. Science fiction makes me feel creepy."

"That's what I like about it."

"Ever since I saw *The Invasion of the Body Snatchers*, I've been practicing leaps when I run, just in case the earth opens up in front of me."

Randy laughed. I laughed. The previous night I had thought I would never laugh again. I licked my cone, considering the offer. "You won't try to hold my hand or anything gross like that?"

Randy made a slight, comical bow. "I promise I'll be the perfect gentleman. Anyway, we aren't going to the passion pit."

I blushed. Teenagers went to drive-ins for just one thing, and it wasn't to watch the movie.

I expected Randy's mom would take us to the theater, but he drove. It was surprising to me that someone in my grade had his license, but Randy had an early birthday, and it seemed that Alice and I always did everything later than other kids. Randy had to sit on a pillow to see over the steering wheel. He made a joke that he was navigating by the stars. He was too short for his age, he acted like a dork, but he seemed perfectly happy with himself. I wondered how you got to that point. Randy paid for me, even though we weren't on a date. Boys always paid for everything. It would be embarrassing for us both if I even offered to buy my own ticket.

On the drive home, he said, "Sorry the movie was so bad."

"It was? I thought I just didn't get it."

He shook his head. "Flying saucers, ghouls rising out of graves—I didn't see the connection."

"I didn't know they had so many drapes in spaceships." I was actually having fun. Whole minutes went by without my thinking of Kenneth, his mouth, my breast, the humiliation. When we got home, the lights were still on in my living room, but Randy's house was black except for the porch light.

"The keepers' bridge night," Randy explained. "Here's your chance if you still want it."

I knew what he was talking about. "I've been dying to take a look."

"I'm warning you. It's nothing special."

"I want to see."

Randy got out of the car, opened the garage door, and drove in. We went through the garage to the backyard. There were lots of stars, but only a thin slice of moon. Once our eyes got used to the dark, Randy led me across the lawn to the little plaster igloo, gleaming white. He reached under a planter and extracted the key.

"Let's make it snappy," he said anxiously. "If my mom catches us, I'm dead." He unlocked the shelter door. I followed him down a narrow staircase, holding onto the wall. Randy lit a kerosene lamp set on a table with a red-and-white checkered cloth. Bunk beds were attached to one wall and pantry shelves held canned goods, water jugs, a first-aid kit, a kerosene stove, books, magazines, and board games.

"Cozy," I said, even though the air was stale and the dim light cast spooky shadows.

"Home, sweet home." Randy sat cross-legged on the carpet, which covered the hard concrete slab.

I sat opposite him. "If only my family had a neat bomb shelter like this. I'd feel a lot safer. Your mom has thought of everything."

"Yeah, swell. Nuclear winter is supposed to last fifty years or more. You wanna play Monopoly for fifty years? I'd rather run around outside and die of radiation."

"Are we all gonna die, Randy?"

"Maybe, maybe not."

"My dad says the Soviets won't strike because they know we'd strike back."

"Accidents do happen."

We both laughed even though nothing was funny. We ended up staring into each other's eyes. Randy's were slightly magnified behind his glasses, soft and brown.

"Would you kiss me?" I blurted.

His eyebrows shot up. "No joke?"

"If we're all going to die, I'd at least like to know what it feels like to be kissed by someone who cares about me."

"O.K., if you're sure you want me to."

I leaned toward him, closed my eyes, and tilted up my chin. Nothing happened. Seconds seemed to pass like minutes. My eyes had been shut so long, my lashes fluttered. Didn't Randy have the nerve to do it? Didn't he want to? I felt the light pressure of his dry lips brush against mine. I opened my eyes.

He looked proud and expectant. "How was it?"

"All right."

"No fireworks?"

"Not really. You?"

He shook his head. "It's because we're just friends." He tapped his temple. "Sex is all in the mind. That's what Hugh Hefner says."

I had never heard a boy say the word "sex." I was certain it was too dark for Randy to see my blush. "Who's Hugh Hefner?"

"He makes *Playboy* magazine."

"Oh." I knew it had naked ladies in it called centerfolds.

"Donna? Do you suppose Brenda would go out with me?"

I tried to let Randy down easy. "If I were you, I wouldn't waste my time on that stuck-up phony."

"I didn't think so." Randy dropped his eyes.

I could see that he was hurt. "Come on. Let's beat it out of here before your mom gets home."

Randy didn't budge. "Donna?"

"Yeah?"

"Have you been kissed by someone who *didn't* care about you?"

"*No!*" I exclaimed in alarm. "Why would you say a dumb thing like that?" I jumped to my feet, blew out the lamp, and groped my way toward the exit.

Behind me in the pitch-dark, Randy spoke in an even, sure tone. "Something happened to you."

CHAPTER SEVEN

One July night, when it was too warm to get to sleep, Alice let out a long sigh and grumbled, "I'm dreading camp!"

I rolled over to face her in the darkness, my head propped up on my elbow. "Why?"

"There's nothing to do. Every year, I just sit in the dirt and wish it were over."

"Really? I thought we always had a swell time."

Camp was what we called getting together with Mom's family on our grandparents' property in Guerneville on the Russian River. Mom had two sisters, Aunt Lillian and Aunt Irene. Aunt Lillian and Uncle Howie lived in San Diego and had four sons, all grownups with families of their own living in different parts of California. Aunt Irene and Uncle Clyde lived in Portland, Oregon, and had one adult daughter, Gladys. Everybody who could manage it showed up to camp each year.

"Sure it was fun when we were little," said Alice. "I'm too old for camp now."

"Do you think Grandpa and Grandma are too old for camp?"

"It's different for them. They're the patriarch and matriarch of the family." Alice let out another deep sigh and rolled over.

The next evening at the dinner table, she complained to our parents, "I hate camp! Those squares don't dig me, and I don't dig them."

Mom's eyes grew wide and round. "Grandma and Grandpa, your aunts and uncles, and all your cousins—you don't like any of them?"

Alice blushed and sputtered, "I didn't say 'like.' I said 'dig.' I hate the way Aunt Irene picks everybody apart."

"Why would you care what Irene says?" asked Dad. "Irene can't help being Irene."

Mom grinned at Dad. "And Howie can't help being Howie."

"And Gladys can't help being Gladys," I joined in.

Alice pushed her chair back furiously. "And Alice can't help being Alice, dig?"

The arguments continued until the afternoon before our departure. Mom was pulling out clothing from our chest of drawers as I packed my suitcase. Alice was sprawled on her bed refusing to help. "Leave my stuff alone. I told you I'm not going."

"Don't be silly, dear," Mom said calmly. "Think how it would look to the others."

"I don't care how it looks. Make up some lame excuse. Tell them I've got lots of reading to do for next semester."

Mom dropped a load of underwear and socks on my bed and placed her hands on her hips. "Reading? Is that what you call it? If we let you stay home alone, you'll just run wild."

I got it then. It wasn't so much that Alice didn't want to go to camp; rather, she saw staying home as an opportunity to be on her own.

Mom and Alice battled all afternoon, and when Dad got home in the evening, he joined in the fray. In the end, Alice got her way. The next morning we drove off, the car packed to the hilt, except for the empty space next to me in the big backseat. It felt strange and lonely and kind of sad, our first family vacation without Alice.

At Guerneville, Grandma and some of the others came to greet us as we got out of the car. Grandma was a sturdy, active woman who always wore housedresses, clunky orthopedic shoes, and her blue-rinsed pin curls in a hairnet. She looked old, but it was hard to keep up with her fishing and hiking.

"Hi, Grandma," I said, extending my arms for a hug.

She looked over my head at the vacant spot behind me. "Where's my girl, Alice?"

"She decided she had too much to do," said Mom.

"Is that so?" Grandma furrowed her brow in a way that flustered Mom.

"She's a diligent student," she stammered, "and anthropology is a rigorous major."

"What could she possibly do with an anthropology degree?" asked Aunt Irene. She had tweezed off her eyebrows and penciled them back on in angry angles. "Sit around on some godforsaken island with Margaret Mead and a bunch of savages?"

"Well, well, she'll soon find an upstanding, eligible man who will make her forget all about such things," said Grandma.

"If there are any upstanding, eligible young men left. I hear there's nothing but beatniks running around Berkeley." Irene's orange lipstick emphasized her sneer.

"Ah, now, Irene," said Dad, giving her a big smacker on the cheek. "I do some running around Berkeley myself, and I'm not a beatnik."

Mom poked him in the ribs with her elbow. "You're no eligible young man either."

That made everyone laugh, and after that my grandma hugged me. My cousin Gladys shuffled forward and fell against my body for a hug. She had twisted, atrophied legs from polio and used crutches with armbands on top. "God bless you, Donna," she said. "We are going to have such fun together." She was in her thirties, but still lived with her parents.

Behind my grandparents' house were seven tent cabins, slabs of concrete with wooden frames covered in canvas. Five of the tent cabins were occupied by Aunt Lillian and Uncle Howie and their grown sons and their families. My parents moved into their tent cabin, and I settled into the one next door, which I had always shared with Alice. As I swept the platform of dirt, batted down cobwebs, and stomped on insects, I realized how much I was going to miss her. All our first cousins were grownups, and all the first cousins once removed were little kids. Without Alice, there was no one near my age at camp. Without Alice, I wasn't allowed to take the canoe out on the river or walk into town. Without Alice, there was no one to whisper comments about family members or make funny impersonations of them. Without Alice, I lacked direction when the relatives split up for group activities. Grandma didn't "believe in TV," and having no TV left another gaping hole in my schedule. Two whole weeks loomed ahead, and I already wished they were over.

Still I managed to fall into the routine of camp. We picked wild blackberries and made pies, played dozens of games of Gin Rummy and Scrabble, and listened to Giants baseball games on the radio. We helped

Grandpa with the upkeep of the property, splitting wood, clearing brush, and hauling and spreading gravel and sand on the long private road leading to the main highway. We fished and swam in the river and walked into town to buy Popsicles or licorice whips for a penny out of a big box sitting on the counter in the Ben Franklin.

The relatives talked endlessly about the weather, sports, food, and gags on TV shows, but not politics and religion, nothing that could upset anyone. That summer, most everyone was reading the thick James Michener novel, *Hawaii,* and the relatives discussed the missionaries and the Hawaiians and how they didn't understand each other. "It's not a book I would sit and read to my grandchildren," Grandma said grimly, which immediately caught my interest.

Mom was a different person at camp. She was the little sister, seven years younger than Aunt Irene, and in her pedal pushers, plaid camp shirt tied at the midriff, and blond hair caught up in a ponytail, she looked like a teenager. Dad fit right into Mom's family, joking and laughing with Uncle Howie and Uncle Clyde and the cousins, even though both uncles thought Joe McCarthy was a hero for saving our country from Communism.

I got paired with cousin Gladys. She wore her long brown hair in braids twisted around her head like a halo, and her small Cupid's bow mouth was perpetually turned up in a smile. She was sweet, but boring, always going on about the evangelist Billy Graham. When I complained about getting stuck with her, mom scolded me. "Donna! She spent her childhood in an iron lung!" I imagined how horrible that was without really being able to picture it. Still I gravitated toward the active group of relatives whenever I could, in order to ditch Gladys.

Camp days passed easily; the nights were the problem. Alone in my tent cabin, I lay awake listening to Dad's snoring next door and cousin Johnny and Linda's infant son, Charlie, squalling down the hill. The crickets chirped, the owls hooted, and greedy raccoons thrashed through the garbage bins. It wasn't what was going on around me that prevented sleep, but what was going on inside my head. I couldn't shake the humiliation of Kenneth's sloppy kiss, his hands on my body. Why had I just stood there and taken it? Why hadn't I reacted?

Over and over, I fantasized different versions of the experience. When Kenneth popped out of the bushes, I screamed and dashed toward the house; Dad came out on the porch still holding the newspaper, and the bum ran off. Or when Kenneth reached for me, I stomped on his foot and socked him in the eye. My favorite scenario was that Alice happened to be looking out the window when Kenneth lunged for me. She stormed out the back door, hit him over the head with a frying pan, and never had anything to do with him again.

One afternoon a thunderstorm and downpour kept everyone crammed inside the big house. The little kids played upstairs, the men with their beers and cigars were gathered around the radio in the living room, and the women prepared food in the kitchen. I loved listening to the stories of my mom and aunties. They were all housewives now, but they reminisced about when they used to work during the war. Aunt Irene had her own beauty parlor attached to her house, but had to close it when Gladys got sick. Uncle Howie and Aunt Lillian operated a gas station. While Uncle Howie worked as a mechanic, Aunt Lillian pumped gas. My grandma had a framed photograph of her standing in front of their gas station, dressed in her uniform of white bellbottoms and a peaked hat, meant for a man. My mom was a telegraph operator, working for the army in the Presidio of San Francisco.

"Your mom was nicknamed 'the Ear,'" Aunt Lillian told me as she rolled out piecrust. She was an older, plumper version of my mom, comfortable in camp clothes and no makeup. "Your mom could decipher Morse code faster than anybody."

"It was a scary time," said Aunt Irene. "At any moment we expected the Japanese to land on the California coast and overrun San Francisco."

"Not really!" I exclaimed.

"We weren't sure what was going to happen," said Aunt Lillian.

"I hated the war years." Aunt Irene carefully lit a cigarette with her wet nails spread out. She had just polished them a bright orange to match her lipstick. "We girls couldn't buy silk stockings, so we had to draw seams up the back of our legs with an eyebrow pencil."

"Those were hard times, but they were good times, too," said Mom.

Aunt Lillian touched the back of her hand, leaving a floury imprint. "That's because you were in love." I knew the story. Mom had met Dad one morning while waiting for the ferry. She noticed a lose button on his suit jacket and offered to sew it back on. "The whole family was up in arms with you taking up with a foreigner," continued Lillian, "an older man with a history at that, but Leo turned out to be a regular good egg."

Aunt Irene pointed one of her evil, penciled eyebrows at Mom. "That remains to be seen."

Mom's face flushed angrily. "What's that supposed to mean?"

Aunt Irene's laugh sounded like a seal barking. "Can't you take a joke?"

"A joke? A joke about what?" Mom demanded.

Aunt Irene just waved her splayed fingers.

Suddenly it was too stuffy and too close in the house with all those people. I jumped up from where I was husking corn with Gladys and nearly shouted, "I'm going to walk to the store!"

"In this weather? Whatever for?" asked Mom.

"We could use some baking soda," said Aunt Lillian.

"Your dad isn't going to want to leave his ball game," said Mom.

"I can go by myself," I said. "I'm not a baby."

"I'll go with you," said Gladys.

"Oh, no, that's O.K.," I said. She and Aunt Irene were the two people I most needed to get away from.

Slowly, painfully, Gladys rose up on her crutches. "I can use the exercise."

"Don't be ridiculous, Gladys!" Aunt Irene said sharply.

"Mother, please! I'm not helpless. Come on, Donna. It's only sprinkling now. Let's see if there's a rainbow."

The walk to the store with Gladys dragged on so long I thought I would jump out of my skin. "Are you sure you're O.K.?" I asked.

"Oh, yes," she answered cheerfully. "I only have to think how much Christ suffered on the cross to keep me going."

A jalopy of teenage boys roared past us, one of the boys hollering, "Gimp!"

Embarrassed to be seen with Gladys, I blushed and dropped my head.

She pretended she didn't hear the insult. "Through God's grace and mercy, we can conquer all our tribulations."

I was sick of hearing it. I wanted to argue if God had so much mercy why did she get polio? I pressed my lips together in an effort to keep quiet. I somehow knew that speaking against her religion was the meanest thing I could do to her.

After we bought the baking soda, I slipped into a phone booth, dialed my grandparents' phone number, and asked to speak to my dad. I begged him to come get Gladys and me, complaining that I was too tired to walk back. Of course, Dad and everyone else thought I was trying to spare Gladys more misery. I let them think I was that good.

The last evening at camp, we all gathered on the riverbank for a feast of fresh trout rolled in cornmeal and pan-fried over an open fire, followed by marshmallows, roasted on a stick, burned on the outside and gooey on the inside. Aunt Lillian and my mom tuned up their ukuleles, and we sang into the starlit night, our voices resonating over the flowing water. I knew how to drop the pitch so that my alto voice harmonized with Mom's ringing soprano, even though we never practiced this at home. We sang "You Are my Sunshine," "Ida, Sweet as Apple Cider," "Glow Worm," "By the Light of the Silvery Moon," and "Good-night, Irene." I felt closer to my relatives when I sang with them than in any conversation I had with them.

"How come we never sing any hit songs?" cousin Tommy complained.

Dad leaped to his feet and launched into "Hound Dog," mimicking Elvis Presley, wiggling his hips, swiveling on his heel, and bending low over an imaginary microphone. He knew all the words and all the moves, his German accent and stiff knee making his performance hilarious. The women screamed and faked-fainted, and I laughed so hard I rolled around and got sand in my mouth.

We returned home to the lives we had left behind. Alice was the same Alice. If she had run wild while we had been gone, it hadn't caused any obvious change in her.

Within the pile of mail waiting on the entry hall table was a subpoena for Dad to appear at a hearing before the House un-American Activities Committee, scheduled for May 12-14, 1960, in San Francisco.

"At least I don't have to waste time flying to Washington," said Dad. "HUAC is coming to me."

"You need a lawyer, Leo," said Mom.

"Such an expense, darling, for what? I'm not being accused of a crime, after all, just of being un-American."

On September 13, 1959, the Soviet Union launched Luna-2, the first spacecraft to strike the moon.

"They're getting further ahead of us," said Randy, the next morning on our walk to school.

"Are they going to try to attack us from the moon?" I asked.

"No, but this will heat up the space race."

"What's so special out there anyway?" I asked.

"Believe me, it's important," Randy said seriously. "The last frontier."

A few days later Soviet Premier Nikita Khrushchev arrived in the US for a thirteen-day visit. Maybe the Cold War was warming up or at least thawing. Maybe we would be friends after all and not blow each other off the face of the earth. There was tension between the nations a few days later, however, when Khrushchev was denied entry to Disneyland. He was quoted in the newspapers as saying, "What is it? Is there an epidemic of cholera there or something? Or have gangsters taken over the place that can destroy me? Then what must I do? Commit suicide?" US authorities stood firm, claiming they didn't have the security to protect him at Disneyland.

"That's not it," said Alice, as we discussed the matter over dinner. "The government just wants to punish him for being a commie. No Happiest Place in the World for him."

"I suspect the real reason," said Dad, a forefinger against his nose. His tone was serious, but the glint in his eye gave him away. "The CIA is afraid the Red is going to steal the plans to the whirling teacup ride and build one just like it in the USSR."

CHAPTER EIGHT

For three nights in October, Alice didn't come home. The first morning I found her bed empty, I didn't think much of it, only that she had come and gone as I slept. The second morning I lied to Mom when she asked me at breakfast if Alice had come home, and the third night I packed blankets and pillows in her bed so that it would seem like she was there if Mom checked on her. I don't know why I bothered to cover for Alice. I guess I thought our parents had enough to worry about with the HUAC hearing coming up. If I could fix their Alice problem, I'd be doing them a big favor. No one could actually fix Alice, I knew, but at least I could try to find her before my parents noticed that she was missing.

On Friday after school, I walked over to Cal's campus hoping to run into her. I didn't know her class schedule, but I wandered through the student gathering places, Doe Library, the Memorial Glade, and Sproul Plaza. I walked over to Telegraph Avenue and poked my head into Kip's. It was dead; not even Air Man was around. There was an open mike that evening, but the place wouldn't start filling up until after eight o'clock. I searched a few other coffee houses and shops, but found no sign of Alice or any of her friends.

I used the pay phone in the Rexall to call Mom and tell her I had gone home with Mary Lou, and her mother had invited me to dinner. I didn't feel good about lying to her, but it had to be done if I was going to continue my hunt for Alice. I ordered a tuna sandwich at the lunch counter. I didn't like the sweet pickle relish in it, but I ate it anyway. I had never eaten a meal in public alone and wolfed down my food, self-consciously shifting my eyes. A lady, drinking coffee two stools down, took notice of me. She had shopping bags all around her and was well dressed, wearing a kind of fur with the little animals' heads still on.

I must have seemed guilty because she asked, "Have you run away from home, girl?"

"Me? Oh, no. I live in the dorms. I needed a change from cafeteria food."

"You don't look old enough to be in college."

"Oh, I skipped two grades!"

"Did you?"

"Yes, I'm practically a genius!" The lady's mouth turned down at the corners in irritation or disbelief, and I could have kicked myself. I always went too far in spinning webs of deception. "Well, good-bye!" I said around my last mouthful of sandwich. I left exact change on the counter, not knowing how to tip. I jumped off my stool and dashed outside.

It was dark and a chilly wind had come up from the bay. Telegraph had filled with people. I searched each passing group, but none of them included Alice. It was getting late, and I was forced to give up. If Mom had called Mary Lou's house to check up on me, I would be in double trouble. I reached the nearest bus stop, checked the schedule, and went inside the Orpheus to wait for the bus. There was Alice, sitting at a table with Kenneth and Angela. Unlike Kip's, the Orpheus served alcohol. If I were noticed by the bouncer, he would kick me out. Alice was underage, too, so I guess they didn't check identification too carefully. I pulled my scarf forward and ducked into a group of people standing in the back of the room. I tried to think of what I could say to Alice to get her to come home with me. I didn't want to approach her with Kenneth sitting there. If only she would get up to use the ladies' room, I could talk to her there.

A beatnik with bongo drums finished reading his poem at the open mike. Abruptly Alice stood up, giving me hope that I could follow through with my plan. Then she looked toward the stage and removed a folded piece of paper from her coat pocket. I fervently hoped it wasn't her blood-running-down-her-open-thighs poem.

"What do you think you're doing?" Kenneth asked, loudly enough to make heads turn his way.

"Hang around and find out," said Alice.

"Don't embarrass yourself." Kenneth gripped her forearm, but she shook him off.

Alice walked to the stage, a little unsteadily. She leaned her backside against the bar stool and squinted in the spotlight. She cupped her palm over her eyes and scanned the audience, causing a few people to chuckle. When she tried to speak, her voice was raspy and barely audible. She cleared her throat, with some high-pitched chirping sounds, which caused more laughter. Soon after she began reading her poem, most people lost interest, talking among themselves at their tables. Her soft voice and slightly slurred speech made her difficult to understand. When she finished, two or three people clapped and she murmured, "Thank you."

She returned to her friends, and Kenneth sneered. "What was that?" He scraped back his chair and stalked toward the door.

"Satisfied?" Angela asked her. "You just had to do it."

"I can read my poetry if I want." Still standing, Alice picked up her glass.

"Not in front of Kenny obviously. Didn't you notice how restless he was? He was looking for an out, and you gave it to him. Congratulations. You just wrecked our whole evening."

"Drop dead. I didn't do anything to him."

"You ran him off. You're always running him off. You're a real drag, know that, Alice? I wish you'd go back to your sandbox and leave the adults alone."

Alice threw her drink into Angela's face.

Angela sputtered in shock, then reached up and yanked Alice's hair. Alice reared back to free herself, then clawed Angela's face. Leaping out of her seat, Angela swung a right hook and punched Alice in the eye. The crowd cheered them on as the bouncer reached them in several long strides. He picked Alice up by the waist and dragged Angela by the neckline of her dress. He brushed past me and tossed them out the back door.

I stood frozen in place, unable to figure out how I could have intervened to stop the fight. I dashed after Alice and Angela, but the bouncer extended a stiff arm to block my way. "This is not an exit!"

"But my sister!" My eyes darted to the back door.

"Your sister? Your parents should've taught her some manners."

"They did! They…" How was I supposed to tell this big, burly man Alice wasn't acting anything like the Alice our parents had raised? I turned and wove through the length of the room, dashed out the front door, and ran around the building to the alley.

Alice and Angela gripped each other in a tight bear hug, looking as if they were engaged in a drunken slow dance rather than a battle. Angela shook Alice off and shoved a foot against her hip, causing Alice to fall heavily against the trashcans. Alice rolled off them, landed face down, and was still. Angela started toward her.

I clenched my fists and shouted, "You leave my sister alone!"

Angela looked at me, then back at Alice. She squatted beside her and turned her over. There were eggshells and coffee grounds in her hair. "Poor kid. Out cold." She patted Alice's face. "Come on, now, wake up."

Alice lolled her head and groaned.

"Help me get her up. My place isn't far from here."

Angela and I each took an arm and pulled Alice up. Placing her between us, we half-walked, half-dragged her along. She smelled like garbage. Angela's dress was torn under the arm and her face bore raised welts from Alice's fingernails.

"I need to get her home," I said.

"What a neat idea." Angela rolled her eyes toward me. "First we get her sobered up."

The few blocks we traveled seemed like miles. We struggled to lug Alice up a flight of stairs, her arms flapping and her head swaying like a daisy on its stem. Angela stopped in a dim hallway and propped Alice against the wall. I did my best to hold her up, while Angela unlocked her apartment and flicked on the light.

I thought all beatnik pads were filthy, cockroach-infested dumps, but not Angela's place. The coffee table and end tables matched. The stereo console held a vase of cattails and there was a sunburst clock hanging on the wall. In her compact kitchen was the same grey Formica dinette set we had at home, and on the counter was a set of plastic canisters in graded sizes and shades of pink. Only a small alcove before the bay window was messy, with a typewriter situated on a small metal table, papers strewn around, and handbills tacked to the wall.

"Home, sweet home," Angela announced. She was too old to be a girl, but she wasn't like any lady I knew. Girls usually lived with their parents until they got married, and ladies lived with their husbands and kids.

Angela presented me with an option I haven't even considered. It seemed dauntless.

"Swell place! You live here by yourself?" I had forgotten about Kenneth.

"When I have enough sense to. Come on, in here." Angela heaved Alice over her shoulder like a sack of potatoes, and I followed behind, holding her up so she wouldn't roll off. We passed through the bedroom to the bathroom. Angela set Alice down in the tub and ran a cold shower. When Alice began to scream and flail her arms, Angela turned off the water. In her bedroom, she pulled clothes from dresser drawers and a closet, returned to the bathroom to set them on a glass vanity table next to the tub. Angela removed her tattered dress right in front of me. She had very pale skin, a soft tummy, and big breasts in a pointy brassiere. This was a grown woman's body, not anything like Alice's. Angela slipped into a robe and slippers and rinsed her face at the bathroom sink, leaning toward the mirror to examine the scratches on her cheek. By then Alice had drawn the plastic pink flamingo shower curtain closed, and was dumping her sopping clothes over the edge of the tub.

In the kitchen, Angela measured coffee into the percolator and began mixing pancake batter. I sat on a stool at the counter, my chin propped on my cupped palms, watching her.

"What?" she asked, smiling ruefully.

"Huh?" I felt myself blush.

"You've been staring at me since we got here."

"Oh, sorry. I don't mean to be rude. It's just that you're so…normal. I mean, normal like a regular lady, only not like one, and I was just wondering how you could…" I was going to say like Kenneth, but instead she finished my question with "knock your sister's block off?" Her laugh came out like a snort. "Temporary insanity."

"Are you from around here?"

"Nebraska, originally."

"How'd you end up here?"

"Long story short, I came out to San Francisco for a week's vacation, loved the city, and ended up sticking around. I can't afford the city, so here I am in the East Bay." She flipped the pancakes and pulled plates out of the cupboard.

"Oh, let me help you." I leaped up, grabbed the plates, and put them on the counter. "What else can I do?"

"Set up some TV trays. Let's break the rules and eat in the living room."

"Whose rules?"

Angela laughed. "Nebraska rules, I guess. The ones I was raised with."

"They must be California rules, too. Our parents don't let us eat watching TV either."

"Rules for squares, then. That must be what they are. Why don't you put on a record?"

I went over to the stereo, but didn't find any of the rock 'n' roll singers I knew. Angela just had Classical music and jazz albums. I put on Louis Armstrong and turned the volume low. Alice emerged from the bedroom, wearing a skirt and blouse, which were too big for her, and a towel wrapped around her hair. One of her eyes was swollen shut. She stared at me with her one good eye and exclaimed, "Donna! What are you doing here?"

"Trying to get you to come home."

"Are Mom and Dad worried that I didn't come home last night?"

"Or the night before that or the night before that?"

"Cripes! It's been that long?"

We settled in the living room, eating the fluffy pancakes with maple syrup, and sipping hot, strong coffee. I didn't like the taste, but I liked that Angela treated me like a grownup.

Angela placed a cigarette between her lips and offered the pack to Alice, but she waved it away with her palm. Angela held the cigarettes out to me.

"Angela! She's fifteen!" Alice exclaimed.

"I was smoking by fifteen." Angela lit up and shook her match out.

"I started at fourteen, but that's no reason to corrupt my baby sister."

"I'm Donna," I told Angela.

"Pleased to meet you." She blew out smoke and told Alice, "I dug your poem."

Alice dipped her chin and raised her eyes. "You did not."

"I did. Especially the line, 'candy cane children rocking their horses in gas masks.'"

Alice's hand flew to her mouth, trying to hide the smile behind it. "That sounds so lame out of context. Kenneth loathed my poem."

"He'd like it better if he thought a man wrote it."

"Women can write poetry." I scraped my plate and licked my fork. "There's Emily Dickinson and Josephine Miles and Sylvia Plath."

"She put her head in the oven," said Alice. "No, thanks."

"A *man* drove her to it," said Angela. "I work my fingers to the bone typing letters at the insurance agency all day, then I'm up all night typing Kenneth's poems."

"I type his poems," countered Alice.

Angela slammed her mug down so that coffee sloshed over the rim. She glared at Alice through narrowed eyes. "Oh, no, you don't! He keeps his typewriter here with me."

Alice seemed as surprised as I was about Angela's sudden flash of anger. She raised one shoulder and let it drop. "Can't help it. I do."

"Bug off, Alice! I'm Kenny's muse." She punched her breastbone with her fingertips. "Only I type his poems, dig? I make changes."

I hoped Alice would let it go, but in her eyes was that smug, defiant glint she gave our parents. "I can edit, too. I mean, I go to Cal, and you just went to Heald's Business College. I guess Kenny didn't go anywhere. His spelling is atrocious."

Angela leaped up so violently I thought she was going to attack Alice again. Instead, she stormed over to the typewriter. She raised it off the desk and held it close to her face to read from the paper that was rolled into it. If she hurled it at Alice, she could do some real damage.

"Who cares who types Kenneth's crummy old poems?" I blurted.

Angela let the typewriter drop onto the desk with a loud bang. She whirled around and jabbed a finger toward Alice. "I change more than spelling. His work is my work. I make his poems better. I change his *words.*"

"How come I didn't think of that?" asked Alice. "He ain't no Allen Ginsberg, that's for sure."

Angela reared back as if she'd been slapped. She lifted the typewriter to read from it again, her lips slightly moving. She raised her eyebrows and tilted her head as if something important suddenly occurred to her, like a cake left to burn in the oven. She flung the typewriter onto the desk. It bounced and skidded to a stop dangerously close to the edge. "Goddamn! So why are we wasting our time on him?"

"You have to ask?" Alice pulled off the towel and arranged her pixie cut with her fingers.

"He's a hep cat, but of most the kicks we get is listening to him talk about the kicks he gets."

Alice slapped the arm of the sofa. "Hey, you know, Angie, you're right! What are we doing just sitting on our keisters? Why don't we jump in your car right now and have our ourselves a goddamn *On the Road*?"

Angela shrugged. "I have to be at work Monday morning."

Alice bit a hangnail. "Oh, right-o. I've got class."

"Besides, we'd probably be raped or murdered or something," said Angela. "That's what independent women get in this world."

"Hell, so we're stuck? We gotta just sit here and wait 'til Kenneth gets back to hear about *his* kicks again?"

"I'm getting pretty fed up with Kenny. The way he just scrammed tonight, dumping us both like sacks of shit!"

Alice laughed. "You'd rather have the man in a gray flannel suit so you can pick out your china and silver pattern together? Every day you could live in squaresville, serve the meatloaf, scrub the kitchen, and sit on the sofa with grey flannel and the little ankle biters watching *Ozzie and Harriet*." Alice was describing our mom and her friends. Their lives seemed perfectly fine to me. It's what I expected for myself.

Angela stared out the window at the black night. "Mr. Gray Flannel Suit doesn't sound so bad right now."

The scraping of a key in the lock caused us to look toward the door. A man who wasn't Kenneth stepped into the apartment. He carried a trombone case and had thick blond hair swirled into an elaborate ducktail. He was younger than Kenneth, with a striking cleft chin and watery blue eyes.

"Who the hell are you?" asked Angela.

"I'm Paul. You must be Angela." He set down his case, flung off his pea coat, and tried to hand it to her to hang up.

"What do you want?"

"Kenneth said I could crash at his pad."

"It's my pad. I pay the rent."

"Details, details. Hey, pancakes! I'll take a plate of those!"

"I'll see if there's any batter left." Angela strode up to Paul and extended her hand. "First, the key to my apartment."

Paul slapped the key into her palm. "You are a detail broad. Ken said you were a cool beat chick." He scratched the back of his head, addressing Angela's breasts. "Maybe I got the wrong apartment." He looked over at Alice and me. "Who the hell are you?"

"Cool beat chicks," I said, and Alice giggled.

"You look like children up past your bedtime." He did a double-take on Alice. "Whoa, where'd you get that shiner?"

"Plenty more where that came from," muttered Angela. She swung her hips around the kitchen counter.

Paul watched her bottom go, then followed after her. Angela looked into the bowl of pancake batter and scraped its contents into the trash. "Ah, tough luck. I'm fresh out." She brought the bowl to the sink and ran water into it. Paul hugged her from behind, swaying in a kind of slow dance. "Feisty, aren't ya? I'll have you for dinner instead."

Angela elbowed him back. "Hands off the merchandise."

"Hey, it's cool. Ken is a cat who loves to share."

She turned to glare at him, arms crossed. "You and Ken can drop dead."

Paul took a step back. "Ken told me there's a free-spirited beat chick livin' here. Guess she ain't home tonight."

"Free means I get to choose whom I want to be with. I'm not in the mood, and I wouldn't choose you if you were the last man standing."

Anger darkened Paul's handsome face. "You just blew the greatest opportunity of your life, dolly." He sauntered toward the bedroom. "Sleep on the floor for all I care."

"Get out!" Angela yelled after him.

"Come again?"

"You heard me. Get lost!"

Paul's full lips curled into a smooth smile. "Now don't get your sweet panties in a bunch. I'll be no trouble at all and history in the morning."

Angela stalked across the room, swung open the door, and pointed through it. "Go sleep in front of a bus, why don't, ya?"

"Take it easy." He gathered his trombone and coat on the way out. "Word from the bird, Kenny boy is going to get a bad report."

Angela slammed the door and crossed her arms. "Looks like *Kenny boy* is moving out tonight." She stomped to his typewriter and, balancing it on the sill, cranked open the window. "Watch this. It's all in the timing." We made so much noise rushing to the window and giggling that Angela held her forefinger to her lips. "Shhh!" When unsuspecting Paul passed under the window, she dropped the typewriter behind him, missing him by inches. He took off running as we shrieked with laughter. "Come on, girls, give me a hand," said Angela.

Together we threw Kenneth's clothes, books, papers, records, and bongo drums out the window. By the time every trace of him had vanished from the apartment, we were breathless with exertion and laughter.

Angela wiped her eyes. "I'm beginning to think most beat men don't need women."

"Who would type their poems?" asked Alice.

Angela didn't look like she was joking. "Oh, sure for typing and for sex, but what else? They're more comfortable with other men. If a woman comes along whose willing, a fellow will use her, but then if she wants something for herself, he splits."

"I don't think it's all *that* bad," said Alice.

"Yeah, kid, well you haven't lived as long as I have. Right now, I feel a hundred years old."

Alice and I walked arm in arm to the bus stop. Her eye was still swollen shut and she was limping, but she was smiling just the same. "Gee whiz, Donna, I never would have believed that you'd take to the streets in search of the prodigal daughter." She curled her fingers under her chin in mocked admiration. "I'm deeply touched. I never knew you cared."

"Of course I care, Alice. So does Mom and Dad. It would be nice if you cared about us."

"I know you think I'm a monster, but you'll see how it is one of these days. If you play the game by the keepers' rules, you'll never get to live."

"I pretty much do what I want and follow our parents' rules."

"Oh? And tonight you told them you were doing what?"

"O.K., I lied. I said I was at Mary Lou's, but only because I needed to find you. What were you and Angela fighting about anyway?"

"Bottom line? Kenneth. Now he's all mine." Under the streetlight her face was flushed with happiness. "I'm not like Angela, ya know, running after him for his crummy poetry. You might have noticed my big daddy lover boy isn't too hard on the eyeballs."

"He's a creep."

"You don't know him."

"He made you feel bad about your poem, he sent that wolf after Angela, and he…he's not the least bit handsome. He's…revolting!"

"Baby sister, are you blind? He's sexier than Elvis!"

"Ick! He looks like one of those creatures with a man's body and goat legs and horns."

"A satyr? That's kookie! I'll have to tell him you said that."

"Please don't. Please leave me out of it. Where's he going to live now, anyway? I'm not letting him into our room."

Alice doubled over laughing. "Maybe he and I can move into the keepers' room, and they can sleep on the couch." She knocked her head against mine so hard it throbbed. It was a small price for getting her back.

CHAPTER NINE

Mom nagged Dad until he hired a lawyer. His name was Harry Goldfarb, a trial lawyer, even though Dad wasn't going to trial. He had defended clients in many civil liberties cases, and he often won. He was real old, but still practiced law fulltime. He was bald, stooped, and most of his belly was below his belt. He came over to our house in the evenings to confer with Dad. On his first visit, Mr. Goldfarb reached out to me and extracted a quarter from behind my ear. After that, when he was expected, I didn't answer the door, but I usually found something to do in the kitchen so that I could listen in on their conversation.

One evening, Dad sat in the living room with Mr. Goldfarb, who took notes on a yellow legal pad balanced on his knee. "It's the damnedest thing, Leo. Whenever anyone goes on trial for committing a crime, the person knows exactly what the charge is, but no one subpoenaed by HUAC knows what the FBI has on him in its files."

"It's unlawful," said Dad. "The government is going to have to admit that eventually. How many lives will be ruined by then? Case in point, the Hollywood Ten."

"Oh, it's clearly against the First Amendment," agreed Mr. Goldfarb. "Every American has the right to make any sort of film they want. And as for you, Leo, every professor has the right to address any topic in a university classroom."

"I've got a great extra credit question for the physics quiz I'm giving tomorrow," said Dad. "Are the HUAC hearings constitutional?"

Mr. Goldfarb cleared his throat with a loud *humph, humph.* "Maybe it's best you don't offer extra credit for the time being, Leo."

Dad laughed. "Yes, yes, Harry. I was joking."

Premiering that fall were two TV shows, which became my favorites. One was *Dobie Gillis*, about a teenager who was always trying to get a girlfriend. He only cared if the girls were pretty, and they only cared if he had money to spend on them, which he didn't. Dobie had a beatnik friend named Maynard G. Krebs, who was cute and funny, and nothing like Kenneth. The other show was *Bonanza*, a western about a rancher with three grown sons, which opened with a map burning up. Dad liked the program, too, and we enjoyed watching it together. The three brothers looked nothing alike, but the youngest, Little Joe, was a real dreamboat. Mom liked *Perry Mason*, which was a show aired at the same time as *Bonanza*, so every other week we had to watch that. Perry Mason was a lawyer who never smiled, and the show was just a lot of boring lawyer talk, which always ended in a courtroom scene. Mason always won his case so what was the point of watching?

Berkeley High had hired a new biology teacher, Miss Bunting, the youngest teacher I'd ever seen. She laughed at the kids instead of yelling at them, and she volunteered to start up a new baton twirling team. I had never held a baton, but I went to tryouts because Miss Bunting was in charge. After school that day over forty girls showed up in the gym. Besides regular girls like me, baton twirling attracted the prettiest, most popular girls who weren't cheerleaders. It didn't seem like I would have much of a chance of making the team.

Miss Bunting had changed out of her school dress into shorts and pulled her hair into a ponytail. I had never seen a teacher in shorts, not even gym teachers. She organized us into neat rows, then said, "Now, girls, we'll start with the basics. Hold your baton straight out in front of you, parallel to the floor, and lightly grip the exact center with your right hand. Remember to always keep your fingers on top of the baton."

Brenda's hand shot up. She had had her waist-length hair cut to wear it in the latest pageboy, but her mother had goofed it up by giving her a Toni home permanent, which had turned her head into an unruly ball of frizz.

"Do you have a question, Brenda?"

"Yes, Miss Bunting. Are we going to get to wear cute short skirts with those adorable little white boots?" Several of the older girls giggled. They probably wanted to know the same thing, but only Brenda had the nerve to interrupt the instruction in order to ask.

"We'll order uniforms eventually," answered Miss Bunting. "First we have to learn to twirl. Now make sure the ball of the baton is at your left and—"

Brenda waved her arm wildly. "What about those tall, furry hats?" she blurted out, without waiting to be called on. "Will we get to have those, too?"

Miss Bunting rolled her eyes in a comical expression of fake exasperation. We all laughed, and Brenda surveyed the room with a self-satisfied grin, loving to be the center of attention. "That's called a busby, and yes, it's part of the uniform, but this is going to take a lot more work than looking cute in a uniform. You girls will soon learn the difference between wanting to twirl a baton and wanting to want to twirl one."

Twirling took patience and practice and getting hit on the noggin a few times with your baton or someone else's. Brenda had no natural talent for twirling, frequently cut practices, and gave up after a few weeks. She was the first girl in our set to go steady, and sitting at the Rexall counter looking into Brad Larsen's eyes as they sipped from the same ice cream soda took up a lot of her time. Peggy Jo had to quit because baton twirling got in the way of her accordion lessons. Mary Lou and Carla stayed on, and so did a new popular girl, Linda Preston, who had moved to Berkeley from New York City. She had big brown eyes, a quick wit, and said "cawfee" instead of "coffee." Within a month, the team had dwindled to thirteen girls. Miss Bunting had not cut a single one. She didn't seem to care if a girl was chubby or clumsy. Each one got to decide for herself whether she wanted to be on the team.

I surprised myself by being pretty good at twirling. I didn't have any great natural talent, but I spent a lot of time at it. Between school practices, I brought my portable record player out on the patio and played the theme from *The Bridge over the River Kwai* over and over, marching around my backyard to that happy, whistling tune, twirling and tossing my baton so high it gleamed silvery in the sky. The best moment in twirling was the anticipation of the catch, and when I grew bored in class, I imagined tossing my baton, waiting for it to come down, and felt the same thrill in my imagination.

Of all the girls Linda could choose from, she picked me for a best friend. I didn't know how I was worthy of the honor. I figured she was so new to our school that she didn't know who was part of the in-crowd, and any day she would drop me for someone more popular. Linda and I stood side by side at practices, and we walked home together. She was a hilarious mimic, and when she imitated certain girls on the twirling team, I'd laugh so hard my side ached. She had a keen eye for phonies and girls like Brenda, who thought they were better than everyone else. We were also great fans of Miss Bunting and liked to speculate about her personal life.

"She is so terrif," I said. "Not like a teacher at all."

"Let's cross our fingers she doesn't get married soon," said Linda. "That's what always happens to pretty, young teachers. They get married and their husbands make them quit teaching or they get preggers." She extended her arms out as if she were carrying a beach ball. "Who would want to stand in front of a bunch of teenage boys like that? Big as a house! They would all know she did *it*."

"Don't all married people do *it*?" I asked.

"Not all of them," said Linda. "I overheard some ladies talking at my mom's bridge game, and one of them complained her husband wasn't interested."

Linda and I decided to go to our school's next sock hop together, and afterward she would sleep over. I wore my circle skirt, even though the embroidered names of Ritchie's records on it made me sad. I couldn't bear to listen to "La Bamba" and "Donna" anymore. Hearing Ritchie's voice and knowing he was dead gave me the creeps. Ricky Nelson didn't really grab me. Neither did Paul Anka, Bobby Darin, or Frankie Avalon, although they were good-looking and their music was swell. I was a teen girl adrift at sea without a fab fave.

The surface of the gym floor was easily scuffed by street shoes so that's why we had to dance in our socks. When Linda and I arrived at the gym, we took off our shoes along with all the other kids and left them in such a big heap, I wondered how we all were going to find our own pairs. The school was too cheap to hire a live band, but the cafeteria's jukebox had been dragged in and rigged so that we didn't need dimes to play it.

The gym was crowded with kids, but not many couples were dancing. Brenda was out there, flopping around in Brad's oversized letterman sweater. Linda and I took our places in a long line of girls waiting to be asked to dance. Many of the boys sat on the bleachers, drinking punch and munching cookies, horsing around and jabbing each other.

Both Linda and I had been really excited about the dance. She wore a new dress, red with big black polka dots and oversized black buttons down the front and at the pockets of the full skirt. She had a cute figure, extra cute that night. She had confided in me that she had put wads of Kleenex in her bra. After nearly an hour of standing around with no action, Linda and I exchanged forlorn looks.

"This is a drag," she said.

"Don't ya know it?"

"Why don't we ask a couple of boys to dance with us?" she suggested.

I shook my head. Who would want the reputation of being a boy chaser? "Boys are supposed to do the asking."

"We could at least try."

I imagined some boy telling me, beat it, skag. "They might say no," I reasoned, "and then I'd wish the floor would open up so I could drop through."

"Pooh, why so dramatic? It would only mean they were bashful. Boys are as insecure as girls, you know."

"They are?" I'd never thought of that.

Linda nodded toward the boys on the bleachers. "Why do you think those boys aren't asking any girls to dance?"

"Fear of rejection?" I suggested.

"Fear of girls! Probably their mothers made them come." Linda shoved her hands in her pockets, rolled her shoulders, and lowered her voice. "Ah, gee, Mom, do I hafta?"

I laughed.

"Hey, I know. We could dance together!"

I looked around the room. Every girl had a boy partner. I gave Linda a look, one side of my upper lip raised.

"Well, Cripes, I wanna do something!" Linda's wide eyes shone with mischief. She took a running starting and skidded in her socks about three feet. "Let's see you top that, Don!"

I gave it a try and sailed past her.

"Oh, yeah?" Linda ran and skidded the other direction.

We began to draw an audience. A few other kids joined us. I skidded into a boy I'd never seen. He caught me by the elbows, laughing. "Wanna dance?"

In the next minute, Linda was dancing, too. In fact, we danced with different partners the rest of the time.

After the sock hop, we talked and giggled together in the back seat, while Dad drove us home. "That was swell," said Linda, "but my feet hurt."

"Too much dancing?" asked Dad.

"No," said Linda, lifting one black-and-tan saddle shoe onto her knee. "My shoes are too small for me."

"What do ya mean *your* shoes?" I asked.

"Whoops," said Linda.

We about died laughing.

During baton practice one day in late October, after our lasso straddles, double leg rolls, and leg-to-leg whips left us panting, Miss Bunting told us to get a drink at the fountain in the foyer and come sit on the gym floor.

"Now, I'm not going to promise you anything, girls, but…." She raised a forefinger in caution. "if you continue to work this hard, and if we can get a simple routine down *and* our uniform order comes in time, we'll be able to lead the marching band in the Christmas Lane Parade."

We whooped and cheered.

Miss Bunting smiled wide. "Now here's what I have in mind. Up! Up! Back to work." She arranged us in three rows of four with Mary Lou marching point, since she was the most coordinated and rarely botched a toss.

By the time the uniform order arrived, we were running smoothly through our routine. Depicting our school colors, the uniform had a gold flared skirt that hit mid-thigh and a tight-fitting red military jacket with gold braid trefoil trim, frog fasteners, and epaulets. The white boots came to mid-calf and had red tassels, and the busby was gold with a red plume. We took our team picture standing in a row with a three-quarter turn, our right knee cocked toward the camera and our silver batons cradled in our left arms.

I loved to put on my uniform and strike poses in my bedroom mirror. I even wore it when I practiced in my own backyard.

"You'll round out the heels of those boots," Mom fretted.

"Oh, let Donna enjoy the costume," said Dad.

"Uniform," I corrected him.

Linda invited Miss Bunting and all the girls on the team to a Christmas tea after the parade. I wondered why it wasn't called a lunch instead of a tea, since it would be held around noon, and I didn't know of any girl who actually drank tea. Linda and I had spent a lot of time together, and she had been over to my house several times, but I had never been invited into hers. She kidded around about how her mother decorated their house just for show, and that no one, not even her family members, was allowed to sit on the furniture. This made me very curious to see the inside of Linda's impressive house on Eunice Street with the two stone lions poised in front, which, Linda joked, her mother had stolen from the front of the New York Public Library.

At practice one day, Miss Bunting let Linda take the time to organize a "Secret Santa." Each of us drew a name of another girl on the team so that we could give her a gift at the tea. I drew Carla's name and Mary Lou got Linda's. Mary Lou and I swapped so we could each have our best friend's name. Mary Lou's eyes met mine as we exchanged the little slips of paper, and I knew instantly we were thinking the same thing: at one time *we* had been best friends. I felt a little nostalgic, but then we grinned at each other, happy to have the name we truly wanted.

Every evening after dinner, I worked on a little booklet, writing and illustrating Linda's funniest jokes, which I titled "Linda Says." I couldn't wait to see the look on her face when she saw it, and then we would have a blast reading it together. The parade and tea was the biggest thing I had to look forward to.

On Friday, after our final practice, Linda was real quiet on our walk home. She had dropped her baton twice during our routine, and I figured she was upset about it.

"It's not the end of the world if someone goofs up at the parade. I mean it's not like your baton explodes like an H-bomb if it touches the ground." I nudged her with my elbow and erupted with a loud guffaw, but Linda wasn't laughing with me this time. "Hey, what's wrong? Did someone steal the stone lions from the front of your house?"

"Gee, Donna, I don't know how to tell you this." She was staring straight ahead. "It's about the Christmas tea."

"What? We gotta bring our own chairs so we won't mess up your mother's furniture?"

"My mother says you can't come," she blurted.

"Why not? Oh! *Oh!*" I wanted to run all the way home and tear the book I had made Linda into a thousand pieces, then fling myself face down on my bed and cry and cry. But I also didn't want to show Linda how much I cared. "It's O.K.," I said lightly. "I probably couldn't make it, anyway. I got a lot of stuff to do tomorrow." My vision was getting blurry so I stopped walking and pressed my fingertips into my eyes. I wished Linda would go on by herself without my asking her to. I felt her picking at my sweater sleeves, gently pulling my hands from my face. Her brown eyes were very round and serious. "I don't care if your dad is a communist. You're still my best friend, Donna."

I shook her hands off me. "My dad is *not* a communist."

"He sure talks like one, with that thick German accent he has."

"That would make him a Nazi."

"He's a Nazi, too?"

"How could you be so dumb, Linda?" I bolted, my mind rushing ahead, making plans. I couldn't tell my parents about this, of course. And I couldn't go to the parade either. All the girls would wonder why I wasn't at the Christmas tea afterward. I would have to miss the parade, and that would goof up our formation. Mary Lou would have to march in my place, and all the girls who depended on point to follow the routine would be lost. Batons would be dropping and rolling like crazy. All of Miss Bunting's and the team's work would go down the drain. Linda would know why. Her mom would see what trouble her excluding me had caused.

The next morning, Mom poked her head into my room to say, "Donna! You've overslept! Hurry up, now. Today's the big day."

I groaned and rolled over. "I don't feel good."

"What? Oh, dear!" Mom strode across the room. She already had on her tweed wool slacks, cashmere sweater set, and silk scarf, dressed for the cold. She pressed her hand against my forehead. "No fever, thank goodness. It's probably just butterflies in the tummy. You'll feel better after some warm oatmeal."

I groaned. "I'll throw up if I eat breakfast."

Alice released an impatient huff and thumped her pillow. She was sitting up in her bed reading *Madame Bovary*, and our conversation was obviously distracting her. Mom looked over at her, then back at me, running her fingers through my hair. "What can I do for you, sweetie?"

"Call Miss Bunting. Tell her I'm sick."

Mom glanced up at my uniform, hanging over my closet door, then back at me. "If you're sure…"

I faked a retching sound and dashed toward the bathroom. I slammed the door, filled a cup with water, and made another retching sound as I flung the water in the toilet. I flushed, shuffled back to my room, and fell into bed. Alice watched me through narrowed eyes. "You're faking."

"Why would I?" I pulled the blankets over my head.

"Beats me. Why don't you spill the beans?"

I heard the bedsprings creak as Alice leaped from her bed. She tore off my blankets, fell on top of me, and pinched my cheek with a painful shake. "Look at that rosy complexion! The very bloom of good health!"

I flailed my arms. "Get off me or I'll barf all over you."

"Not 'til you 'fess up."

"O.K.!" I sat up, panting.

Alice grinned. "Quite a hearty fight you put up for such a sickee. What's cookin'?"

"Oh, it's Linda's stupid mom," I admitted. "She says I can't come to the tea, and I'm too embarrassed to go just to the parade."

"Why would she exclude you?" Alice pursed her lips and scrunched her brow. "Oh. *Oh!* That narrow-minded McCarthyite bitch!"

My chin wobbled. I dropped my head and raised it back up again.

"Oh, hell, no, Donna! You gotta fight this thing." Alice jumped off my bed and hauled me up by the armpits. "Come on, upsy Daisy."

"Alice, I can't!"

"You bet your little white booties you can!" She tried to pull my flannel nightgown over my head like I was an oversized doll.

"I can dress myself!"

"Get moving then!"

I washed up and put on my uniform. Downstairs I took my car coat from the hall closet, and Mom buttoned me up all the way to my chin.

"I don't know if this is showing good judgment," she said. "Going out in the streets half-dressed and you already sick."

"She's not sick!" exclaimed Alice. For one terrible moment, I thought she was going to expose Mrs. Preston, but she continued with, "You were right about the butterflies, Mom. Donna will be fine once she starts marching. Now, come on, we've got to dash."

It was too late to call Miss Bunting again. Already there was a traffic jam downtown, and Dad had to drop me off several blocks from the staging area. Miss Bunting was surprised to see me, and all the girls were relieved to have me scurry into position at the last moment, which allowed Mary Lou to return to her point position. Linda greeted me and tried to make conversation, but I gave her the cold shoulder. I knew she couldn't pick the mother she had, but right then I was too bitter to be nice to her.

There were dozens of grownups and scads of little kids crowding University Avenue, cheering as we passed. It made me feel real special, as if all of them had come out just to see me twirl my baton in my little gold skirt. A few girls dropped their batons along the way, but not me! I was nearly perfect, hurling my baton high into the sky on each toss. I didn't know if it was the cold, joy, or pride, but toward the end of the parade, tears were streaming down my face, and all I could think was *Alice! Alice! Alice!*

At the end of the route, I found my parents and sister. I pressed my hand to my stomach. "Mom, I can't go to the tea."

"Oh, dear, how will I ever find Mrs. Preston in this crowd to offer your regrets?"

"I already told Linda. Let's just go!"

Mom placed her finger to the side of her mouth. "I'm not sure Emily Post would approve of that."

"It's fine with Emily," said Dad, wrapping his big overcoat over my skimpy uniform. "Let's get Donna out of the cold."

CHAPTER TEN

No one was interested in watching TV with me, so I watched my usual shows alone, missing that cozy feeling of my whole family gathered together in the living room on a winter evening. Dad was upstairs working in his study, and I assumed Alice was in our room doing homework. I wondered why Mom didn't join me.

When I climbed the stairs to go to bed, my parents' bedroom door was closed, with Mom's and Alice's voices murmuring behind it. Mom was crying or was it Alice? I paused to eavesdrop, but Mom called out in a high-pitched, stern voice, "Donna, is that you? Go to bed!" Her voice was so sharp that I immediately obeyed her.

I lay awake, waiting for Alice. She didn't turn on the light, but I could hear her sniffling as she changed into her nightgown.

"What's the matter?" I whispered.

"None of your bee's wax," she said wearily.

"Are you flunking out?"

She breathed out an agitated sigh. "You're so naive, Donna. You think getting a bad grade is the worst thing that can happen to you."

"I do not! Dad being investigated by the FBI is much worse!"

"Yeah, yeah, this family's got big problems."

"What's eating you?"

My sister fell heavily into bed. "Just shut up and go to sleep."

Alice stopped wearing all black and switched to jumpers, white blouses, bobby socks, and saddle shoes, dressing like most of the Cal coeds. In fact, she wore the same blue plaid jumper so often, it was like a uniform for girls who went to Catholic school. She stopped dying her hair black and chopping it off. It looked weird, black with blond roots, until Mom took her to the beauty parlor to get it bleached all blond and styled into a pageboy. Alice mostly wore it pulled back in a stubby ponytail. She hardly ever put on makeup, even lipstick. She stopped going out. She didn't even get together with Darlene or any of her other college friends. She went to class, came home, studied, and read and read.

Alice wasn't a smart aleck anymore. She wasn't Coolsville. She was blank, like those people in *The Body Snatchers,* who have the outward appearance of their usual selves, but are actually programmed by aliens. When she didn't have to get up to go to class, she stayed in bed until nearly noon, munching Sugar Frosted Flakes from the box. Her stack of novels on her nightstand grew, including *Madame Bovary, Anna Karenina,* and *The Awakening.*

One Saturday morning while I was in bed beside her, chuckling over *Fifteen* by Beverly Cleary, tears rolled silently down her face and dripped onto her nightgown. She let out a long, quivering sigh as she came to the last page of *The House of Mirth.*

"Why are all the books you read so sad?" I asked.

"They're all about women who do what the hell they want and end up dead because of it."

"That's depressing! Why don't you read a funny book?"

"I prefer the sad ones."

"Why don't you go out like you used to?"

She shrugged. "I am weary of the world."

That didn't sound like Alice at all. It must have come out of one of her dead lady books. "Aren't you a beatnik anymore?"

She frowned. "Was I ever?"

"You dressed like one. You went out with them. Aren't you dating Kenneth anymore?"

"*Dating?* You mean like going steady and wearing his frat pin?" Alice snapped sarcastically.

"I mean do you get together with him?"

She glared at me. "Does it look like it? He's Gonesville!'"

"Oh. Where'd he go?" I asked lightly, then held my breath. I hadn't gotten this much out of Alice in months.

"Beats the crap outta me! Wherever men who jump into cars with other men go: New York, Mexico, Timbuktu, Gonesville, you dig?"

"Is he coming back?"

"I don't care! I hope he eats shit and dies!" Alice threw down her book and plunged her hand into her cereal box.

So that was it! Alice had been in love with Kenneth, and now she was what Dobie Gillis called "lovesick." Except that Dobie made it seem funny, and Alice was miserable. Her heart was broken. That was what all the hit songs were about. I crossed my arms, blurting, "Well, I'm glad he's Gonesville. He's a creep!"

She looked over at me, her watery eyes blinking once. "Maybe, but there were good things about him, too. He knew how to take whatever he wanted. He knew how to suck the marrow out of life."

"Can't you suck the marrow out of life, too?"

"I tried, but you should know it's not the same for women. Women get *punished* for it!" She looked thoughtfully across the room, then pulled her notebook out from under pillow and began writing.

Our Christmas tree stood naked in the corner of the living room for a whole day, with me clamoring, "When are we going to decorate the tree? When are we going to decorate the tree?" until Mom finally said, "Oh, Donna, just do it yourself."

"By myself? Why can't Alice help?"

"She's busy."

"No, she isn't! She's up there reading."

"It's her Christmas vacation. If that's what she wants to do, let her."

It wasn't much fun hanging ornaments and icicles by myself, but I did it, while Elvis Presley crooned "Blue Christmas" on the stereo, and Mom cut out a new jumper for Alice on the dining room table.

I peered over her shoulder at the pattern envelope, and noticed it was a size bigger than Alice usually wore. Pointing to it, I said, "She sure is gaining a lot of weight."

"It's just a growing spurt."

"She's getting fat, Mom. You know it!"

She released a puff of air. "Don't say anything to her about it, Donna. Food can be a comfort when nothing else is."

"Do you think she'll ever get over him?"

"Who, sweetie?"

"You know, Mom. Kenneth! The boy—man—she's mooning over."

"Oh, Donna, I don't think it's any one boy. It was that whole crowd of beatniks she ran around with. They weren't very nice to her, and she's disillusioned. She thought they had some answers for her, and they didn't. Give her some time. She'll find her way."

I nodded, but I wasn't at all satisfied with Mom's explanation. Did she really believe it herself? How could she not know about Kenneth? I was pretty sure that's who Alice was talking about when I had overheard her crying on Mom's shoulder. It wasn't the first time I thought my mom pretended to know less than she actually did.

Three Santas showed up at my parents' holiday cocktail party. The skinny one with the black beard was Dr. Tucker, the fat one whose fake white beard kept slipping off his heavy jowls was Dr. Aldridge, and I didn't know the third one. There were lots of jokes about red-baiting the Santas in their red suits.

Dr. Tucker joked, "It's true, you know, that McCarthy was able to disclose the names of two million communists."

"I always believed old Joe was onto something," said Dr. Aldridge. "How'd he do it?"

"He got his hands on the Moscow telephone directory."

"I've got a good one," said Mrs. Tucker. "Three Soviets met in a labor camp. The first one said, 'I was arrested because I was ten minutes early for work and was accused of espionage. The second one said, 'I was arrested because I was ten minutes late for work and accused of sabotage.' The third one said, 'I was arrested because I was on time for work and accused of possessing an American-made watch.'"

My favorite joke was told by the lady poet. "The American ambassador to the Soviet Union was named Rudolph. He and his wife took Nikita Khrushchev to an American football game. Khrushchev held out his hand and said, 'It's raining.' The ambassador said, 'No, it's sleeting.' His wife leaned toward him and said, 'Rudolph, the Red knows rain, dear.'"

My parents' guests enjoyed the jokes about Communism and McCarthyism, but not so funny were Mrs. Preston excluding me from

Linda's tea and Dad having to appear before HUAC in May. The day after her holiday party, Mom didn't get out of bed. We stepped over plates of leftover food, overflowing ashtrays, and lipstick-smudged glasses until around four in the afternoon, when Alice and I began to slowly pick things up, fill the garbage can, and wash the dishes.

A few days after New Year's, we were all watching *Leave It to Beaver*, Alice and I sharing a bowl of popcorn on the sofa.

Mom set down the department store sales section of the newspaper and began rubbing one hand over the other in a circular, washing motion, a habit she'd recently developed. "Winter coats are on sale at the Emporium, Alice," she said. "You'll need one in Oregon."

"Oregon?" I repeated. "Are we going to visit Aunt Irene? How come no one told me?" Alice gripped a fistful of popcorn, but didn't raise it to her mouth. I wanted to reach into the bowl myself, but couldn't get around her hand.

"We're not all going, Donna," said Mom. "Just Alice."

I raised one side of my upper lip. "Why?"

Mom's hands twirled more rapidly. It seemed she wasn't going to answer me, but then she blurted, "Gladys has suffered a relapse of polio. Alice is going to help Aunt Irene take care of her."

"But how would you have time, Alice?" I asked. "School starts next week."

She squeezed the popcorn in her hand, staring vacantly across the room with her *Body Snatcher* expression.

"Alice won't be attending college spring semester," said Mom.

"You're dropping out!" I looked over at Dad, who remained silent, hidden behind his newspaper. Did he even hear what was going on? How could he allow it?

"It's just a leave of absence," said Mom. "She'll catch up on units in the summer and fall, won't you, Alice?"

"Don't go!" I exclaimed. "Gladys is a real drag! All she talks about is Billy Graham and Jesus Christ, her personal savior."

"Donna!" exclaimed Mom, "Gladys is deathly ill."

"I'm sorry. Can't Aunt Irene hire a nurse?"

"In a family we help each other out. That's what families are for."

I rolled my eyes up at Alice. "Aunt Irene will drive you bonkers. You know how she is."

Dad's newspaper came down in a crumpled heap on his lap. "Donna, that's enough!" His sharp tone caused my scalp to prickle. He reached over to still my mother's hands. They were chapped red from the constant rubbing. Dad sometimes joked that Mom was his Lady Macbeth, but no one was goofing around now.

A strange stillness settled over my family, which I didn't understand. Arrangements had been made without me. Things must be worst than I thought, and I had been sheltered from them. "Oh, Mommy, is Gladys going to have to go back into the iron lung?"

Beneath Dad's broad hand, Mom's hands stirred. "I'm not certain. I believe so."

Alice dashed the handful of popcorn against the bowl and stomped out of the room.

When I went up to bed, she pretended to be asleep, but she didn't fool me. "Just tell them you won't go," I hissed. "They'll eventually have to listen to you."

"Oh, Donna, I have to get out of here."

So Alice was going willingly, even though that was not how it had seemed to me. Maybe her trip to Oregon was supposed to help her forget Kenneth. "You need a change of scenery?"

Alice snorted. "That's a good one. Right-o."

That week Alice packed two huge suitcases. I was in school and Dad was at the university when Mom drove her to the train station in Emeryville. When I got home that afternoon, Alice's half of our room was cold and empty, stripped of her personal belongings and dead lady books; the typewriter on our desk was latched in its case. I had dreamed of having a room of my own some day, but now that I had it, I yearned for Alice. I happened to glance down at the wastebasket and found her notebook of poems there. I plucked it out and placed it between my mattress and springs along with her other writing.

CHAPTER ELEVEN

"Write your note to Alice, Donna, so I can get this week's letter off." Mom was still in her magenta silk pajamas and pink lacy bed jacket. It was a Saturday morning, and she and I were seated at the breakfast table.

I stared at the daffodils blooming in the backyard, my chin in my hand. "Pooh, she never writes back!"

"She does sometimes." In one letter, Alice would state that Gladys was improving, and in the next, that she had suffered a relapse. She wrote how grateful Aunt Irene was for her help. She closed each letter with a weather report, mostly rain.

"I want her to write back just to me!"

"Why, Donna, that would be wasting a stamp."

"No, it wouldn't!" It would be worth a juicy letter filled with Alice's sarcasm and wit. I wanted to know what was *really* going on between her and Aunt Irene. They didn't even like each other.

Mom rubbed her temples. She had dark circles under her eyes. Although she spent many hours of the day and night in bed, she complained of insomnia. "I know what we'll do. Let's make sugar cookies."

"In March?"

"We'll use the bunny cookie cutter, for Easter."

"No, thanks." I knew Mom didn't really want to bake cookies. She barely had the energy to fry the egg that was untouched and cold on her plate. "Want me to get you the aspirin bottle?" I offered.

"No, sweetie, I'm O.K. Just tired."

"It's more than that. Maybe you should go to the doctor."

"I am seeing a doctor, a psychiatrist."

"You are?" This was the first I'd heard of any headshrinker. Weren't they just for crazy people? "Does he give you pills?"

"No, darling. We just talk."

"What does he say is wrong with you?"

Mom stared at her cigarette, burning down to a thin tube of ash. "He says I have a nervous disorder."

"Because of Dad's HUAC hearing?"

"I don't know why. Mr. Goldfarb is taking good care of Daddy. I guess I just miss Alice." She tilted her head and smiled faintly.

"Remember how she used to slam the front door and stomp up the stairs like she was ready kill somebody?"

"And roll her eyes whenever I suggested she wear something pretty."

"And she called us names—square and that fancy word, too."

"Bourgeoisie."

"What is that supposed to mean?"

"Middle class."

"Well, aren't we?"

Mom shifted her eyebrows. "That's Alice."

"Let's call her!" I exclaimed.

"What for?" Mom's hand trembled slightly as she ground out her cigarette.

"Just to say hi."

"Goodness, Donna, the cost! You don't just call long distance to say hi."

"I bet it would cheer you up, Mommy, just to hear her voice."

"I've got plenty to be cheerful about. I've got you and Daddy. It's a beautiful spring day. Nothing to be sad about at all." She twisted her poor red hands, one over the other. "I know. Let's make cookies!"

I went out to the backyard to practice my baton. Baton-twirling season had ended with the Christmas Lane Parade, but I still liked to twirl on my own. I tossed my baton higher and higher, not really concentrating, thinking about Alice and Mom. My baton smashed into a branch and ricocheted into the Greenes' backyard. I heard a howl and a long, low groan. It took me a moment to realize Randy was faking that he got hit. I leaped up onto a cement planner to lean over the fence. "Hand it over."

Instead of passing my baton to me, he ran out his gate and through mine. He had just gotten a crew cut, but his baby fine hair didn't stand up the way it was supposed to. "Hey, teach me a few moves."

He wasn't kidding. Some of the things Randy did embarrassed me, and if he had any sense, they should embarrass him, too. "Boys don't twirl batons."

"They sure do! Haven't you heard of a drum major?"

"Only majorettes. Don't you even care if people call you a sissy?"

Randy tried to pass the baton from one hand to the other. "I guess if I were a sissy I'd care. What's a sissy, anyway?"

I planted my hand against my hip. "Randy, you know, just like everyone else: a boy who does girl things. Here, you're doing it wrong. It's all in the thumb. I'll show you." I took the baton from him, demonstrated an easy hand exchange, and returned it to him.

He repeated it perfectly. "You remember in junior high how Rick Gorecki would pound a boy carrying a violin?"

"Yeah. So?"

"You ever go to the San Francisco Symphony? The violinists are practically all men. You go to a fancy restaurant, the chefs are men. Artists, fashion designers—men. So-called sissies grow up to be men at the top of their professions. Gorecki will be lucky to get a job in the sewer."

I burst out laughing. It was true: handsome, muscle-bound Rick had to take bonehead English. It never occurred to me to imagine what the popular kids or anybody else would be like after high school, but Randy had it all figured out way ahead of time.

It was actually fun teaching him how to twirl a baton. After mastering lesson two, the toss, we paused to drink from the hose and stretch out on the lawn.

I pulled out a handful of grass and tossed it. "Something's rotten in Denmark."

"Yeah? What about?"

"Alice. Why would my dad let her drop out of college to go nurse our cousin Gladys? It makes no sense."

"Do you think she could've gotten kicked out of Cal?"

I reared back, tucking my chin against my throat. "For what?"

"Misconduct? Plagiarizing her papers?"

"Alice writes her own papers. I've seen her. Her report card was straight A's."

"What if you just called her on the phone and asked her what was going on? You think you could get anything out of her?"

"Sneak a phone call?" I slapped my knee. "Terrif! My mom would never find out."

"Yeah, she would. It would be on the phone bill, but if you keep it under three minutes, it won't cost an arm and a leg."

I smiled at Randy. He squinted his eyes, curled his upper lip to bare his teeth, and grinned like a Chinaman. Randy was a weird kid, but I liked him. If he were a girl, he could be a real friend.

The next Friday, I came home to an empty house. It was Mom's grocery shopping day, and I knew I would have some time alone. I sneaked into the den and rummaged in her top desk drawer for her little green address book. As I dialed Aunt Irene's number, my pounding heart told me I was doing something I shouldn't.

When Aunt Irene answered, I said, "Hi, it's me, Donna."

"Donna? Is something the matter?"

"No, nothing. I just called to…" I knew it would be rude to directly ask to speak to Alice. "to see how Gladys is."

"How thoughtful! Would you like to speak to her?"

"Uh…sure." I wondered if someone could talk on the telephone and be in an iron lung at the same time.

"Hello, Donna," Gladys chirped. "God bless you! How are you?"

"Fine. How are you?"

"Fine. How's your mom and dad?"

"Fine."

"How's Alice?"

"Uh…fine." My heart pounded harder. I sort of went limp and had to squeeze the receiver to keep from dropping it. "I have to go now," I blurted, even though I was pretty sure three minutes weren't up.

"But why did you call?" asked Gladys.

"Oh, just to see how you were doing."

"Well, I'm fine. We had a fabulous time together at camp, didn't we?"

"We sure did. Good-bye, Gladys."

"Toodle-oo, Donna. Thank you for calling."

I wanted to dash over to the Greenes' to blab to Randy, "*She's not there!*" but I resisted. If Alice's whereabouts was kept a secret from me, maybe no one else was supposed to know either. I went upstairs and lay on my bed, staring over at Alice's vacant side of the room. She wasn't at Aunt Irene's, so where was she? My parents—my mom, at least—had lied to me. Why? I could confront her about it, but something told me not to. Maybe Alice had committed a terrible crime and had been sent to prison, but that didn't seem right either. She'd have to have a trial first. I slammed my fist into my pillow. How would I ever find out the truth?

A few weeks later, walking home from school up Spruce Street, I could see the little red flags sticking up from the mailboxes. This was unusual; the mailman was late. I opened our mailbox and peered in. There was nothing but paid bills inside, but it gave me an idea. An outgoing letter to Alice would have her address on it. If only I could see one of those, it would solve the mystery of where she was.

I knew where Mom kept outgoing mail inside the house before she put it in the mailbox. On her desk in the den was a holder I had made for her in Kindergarten, a clothespin and a plastic rose stuck into a hairspray cap filled with plaster of Paris. I checked it every day for a couple weeks only to realize Mom wasn't leaving her letters to Alice there.

I was home alone on another Friday, sitting on the sofa eating strawberry ice cream out of the carton, when the doorbell startled me. I looked out the side window at the front door to find the mailman. When I opened the door, he tipped his cap to me and handed me a letter. "No stamp on this one, Miss. You owe three cents." The letter was from Alice, a return address written in her small, neat penmanship:

> Miss Alice Kronenberger
> Samuelson Maternity House
> 423 Maddox Street
> Mountain View, California

I don't remember finding three pennies and handing them to the mailman, but I must have. I sat on the edge of the couch and stared at the pale blue letter resting on my knees. I'd heard of maternity clothes and maternity wards in hospitals. A maternity house must be for ladies who were going to have babies. Why would Alice drop out of college to go work there, and why was it such a big secret? Maybe she wasn't working there. Maybe she had gone there to…

Impossible! I knew girls could have babies without getting married, but only if they had sexual intercourse. Some girls went all the way with boys before they got married, but only bad girls, cheap girls, easy girls, not good girls from good families like Alice. There was always gossip going around about girls at our school who were doing it, but I didn't believe it. Boys always wanted to do it, but it was painful for girls and it ruined their reputations. If a girl lost her virginity, no boy would want to marry her. If she got pregnant, it would disgrace her and her family. The boy could try to fix things by quickly marrying the girl, but then the baby would come before they had been married nine months, and that would bring shame to the family. If the couple didn't marry, then the girl had to go away and…

Not Alice!

Mom came through the back door loaded down with groceries.

I shoved Alice's letter in the waistband of my skirt and pulled my blouse over it. "Oh, hi, Mom." I went out into the garage, lifted two bags of groceries out of the trunk, carried them into the kitchen, and set them on the counter.

When Mom looked into my face, her jaw slackened. "Oh honey, what's wrong?"

"Nothing!" I felt the heat of a blush rise to my hairline.

She pressed her hand to my cheek and gazed kindly into my eyes. "Something is."

I burst into tears. "Oh, Mommy, I got an F on my geometry test! Don't tell Dad!"

"It's not the end of the world."

"Yes, it is!" I ran upstairs to my room, shut the door, and sat on the floor against it so that I couldn't be disturbed. I ripped open the letter. Alice didn't have much to say as usual. She was fine. She was learning to knit. It was raining. I threw myself on my bed face down and cried into my pillow.

"Donna! Donna!" Mom yelled up at me in a strident tone. "Why is a carton of ice cream melting all over the living room carpet?"

If no one would tell me what was going on with Alice, I would find out for myself. I knew menstruation had to do with pregnancy, but only because Brenda told me it did. During one sleepover in the sixth grade, she had told Mary Lou and me what sex was. I was shocked that my parents and other grownups who had children would do such a thing, but when I got home from Brenda's and asked Alice about it, she said it was true. When I had asked her more questions, she waved me away, saying I was too young to know anything more.

I got up from where I was sitting against the door and rummaged through the bottom desk drawer for the Kotex booklet my mother had given me when I was in eighth grade and had my first period. Just as I remembered, it didn't offer much information: "Once a month, for just a few days, your body will get rid of a small amount of blood and tissue it doesn't need. These fluids leave through the vagina, an opening you have in the lower part of your body." I tossed the booklet aside in disgust. Not a thing about sex or pregnancy. I wanted to know how a baby could grow inside my sister.

Saturday morning, I walked over to the library. I knew all the books about sexual intercourse were on reserve, and you had to be eighteen to check them out for an hour. I wandered through the stacks and found the anatomy section. I took several books off the shelf, one by one, and flipped through them. There were lots of illustrations of the human body, but none of a pregnant female. I came across a close up of male genitals, which sidetracked me. I twisted the book on its side to get a better look, trying to figure out how a boy could put that floppy thing inside a girl, when I heard a sudden, hushed voice, close to my ear.

"May I help you, Miss?"

I started. The book I was holding leaped in the air and fell to the carpet.

A stern-looking librarian glared at me through black cat-eye glasses, her lipstick seeping into the creases above her upper lip.

"Uh, I'm just looking."

"I can see that."

I hid my blush by stooping to pick up the book I had dropped. I slid it back where I had found it.

"Do not reshelf!" the librarian snapped, pointing to a sign. She took the book out of its place, read the number on its spine, and replaced it where I had put it. "Now what exactly are you looking *for*?"

I put my hands behind my back and tightly twisted my fingers together. "I have a report to do on…the human body."

"In the summertime?"

"For summer school," I said, even though I was certain she knew I was lying.

Her nostrils flared as she puffed air through them. "Let me show you where the encyclopedias are." I followed her across the room. "There," she said, gesturing toward a lower shelf. "We have the Britannica and the World Book."

"Thank you, ma'am."

"And don't copy!" She narrowed her eyes at me. "Where's your binder?"

"I was just going to check out—"

"You can't check out encyclopedias!"

"Yes, ma'am. I'll read it here." I bent over, reaching for the A volume of the red leather World Book. When the librarian got busy at the circulation desk, I sneaked back to the nonfiction stacks and found exactly what I was searching for. I crept to the study area, sat at a carrel, and opened the book. There it was, an illustration of a baby all curled up, caught mid summersault within a pink lining inside a woman's body, its head pointed down toward a tiny tube between the woman's legs. *How could a whole baby fit through that?* The book rose up into the air and closed with a slap.

The crabby librarian was bent over me, poking me painfully in the shoulder. "Huh! I knew you were up to no good, and now I've caught you red-handed. Do your parents know you have an interest in smut? I've a good notion to telephone them right now. What's your name, girl?"

"D-donna."

"Donna what? You have a last name, don't you? When people ask you your name, have the sense to state your full name."

"Donna…Smith."

"Come with me, Miss Smith."

I followed her to the circulation desk and got the satisfaction that her slip was showing in back.

"You'll never guess what this one was poking her nose into," she muttered to a younger librarian who was stamping the date on the little paper inside a book.

The woman cringed, trying to take up less space than her ample bosom would allow. "Was it…was it *Peyton Place?*"

"Worse!" The cranky librarian selected the telephone directory from the back shelf and opened it to the many pages of Smiths. "What is your father's name?"

"George," I stammered, the first boy's name that came to my mind. "I mean, George Smith."

"Well, obviously." When she bent closer to read the fine print, I made a dash for the door. "You impertinent girl," she called after me in a stage whisper, "Stop this instant!"

I didn't slow down until I reached my own front steps.

CHAPTER TWELVE

With its rolling lawns, fountains, rose gardens, and statuary, the Woodbridge Sanatorium looked like a lavish park or a cemetery for rich people. I especially liked the walking path through a miniature village inhabited by plaster animals and grinning gnomes. Mom had been driving up to Santa Rosa to Woodbridge on her own since late January for biweekly appointments with her psychiatrist, Cedric Friedman. This was a Saturday, however, and Dad and I were accompanying her. I had never heard of a doctor's appointment on a Saturday.

Mom led us to the largest building on the property and down a wide carpeted hall with armchairs situated outside each doorway. She knocked at one of the rooms, and a little man in a brown suit answered. He had a pointy beard, rimless spectacles attached to a cord, and hair parted just above his right ear, thin strands combed over his shiny head.

Mom smiled at him and offered her gloved hand. "Good morning, Dr. Friedman. This is my husband, Dr. Kronenberger, and our younger daughter, Donna."

Dr. Friedman bowed slightly and extended his arm toward the inside of his office.

"Wait out here, Donna," said Dad.

I was tired of being left out of things. "I want to come, too."

Dad's smile was small and tight, a kind of warning. "This is grownup talk,"

I straightened my spine and lifted my chin. "I am grown up, just about. I'm fifteen!"

Mom placed a light hand on Dad's sleeve. "Let her in, darling. If I'm going into the nut house, Donna has a right to know why."

I gasped. "You're going to stay here? Why?"

"That's what we're going to find out," said Mom.

We entered the wood-paneled room. I strolled the perimeter, gawking at gold-framed photographs of Dr. Friedman and famous people: Judy Garland, Marlon Brando, Dick Clark, and a bunch I didn't know. He was shorter than all of them, and in each picture he had different amounts of hair.

After we were seated, Dr. Friedman opened a file folder and shifted the papers in it. "The results of the examinations are in, and I have a diagnosis. Mrs. Kronenberger is suffering from a manic-depressive reaction brought on by both biogenic and social factors."

There was a lot I didn't understand in that sentence, but I clamped down on the questions I had.

"What is the proposed treatment?" asked Dad.

"Complete, undisturbed rest—"

"Mom can take naps at home," I blurted, "every day, if she wants. I won't disturb her, I promise."

"That's very thoughtful of you, Miss Kronenberger," said the doctor. "However, rest at home is not nearly as effective as being admitted into a nervous hospital. Mrs. Kronenberger must be removed from the environment that is causing her abnormal agitation and begin a therapeutic regimen."

Dad waved his palm. "No narcotics are to be administered."

Dr. Friedman reared his head back. I could tell he wasn't used to being told what to do. "Certainly if Mrs. Kronenberger becomes overly anxious or has trouble sleeping..."

"No. No antidepressants or sedatives," Dad insisted sternly. "If you make a narcotic addict of my wife, I will hold you legally responsible. If Mrs. Kronenberger agrees to admission, she will be here for a rest cure, nothing more."

Dr. Friedman seemed to be completely engrossed in emptying out his pipe. Finally, he looked up. "I agree rest is key to Mrs. Kronenberger's condition, but without some further treatment, I can't guarantee a full recovery. There are, of course, alternatives to prescribed medications."

"Such as?" Dad prodded.

Mom leaned into Dad. "Dr. Friedman and I have been discussing the possibility of electroshock therapy."

Dad's face grew long and serious. He looked over at me.

"It's perfectly all right for Donna to hear this." Mom nodded encouragingly at the psychiatrist. "Dr. Friedman, please explain the procedure."

"Simply, we place electrodes at the temples and administer a mild electric shock to the brain that results in a seizure—"

"An induced epileptic convulsion?" asked Dad. "I thought such barbaric treatments were abandoned in the dark ages!"

Mom placed her hand on Dad's arm. "I've read about this, Leo. I've spoken to some of Dr. Friedman's patients who have had the treatment. It does help some people."

"I saw it in a movie once," I piped up enthusiastically. "That's how Frankenstein brought his monster to life!"

"Hollywood nonsense!" Dr. Friedman exclaimed. "I'm talking about an internationally accepted medical treatment, which has been much improved over the years of its use."

"I don't like the sound of it," said Dad. "How do you prevent patients from harming themselves throughout the convulsion?"

"The patient it completely safe. We administer a mild muscle relaxant and place a mouth guard between the teeth."

Dad furrowed his bushy brows. "What does it do to the brain?"

Dr. Friedman tried to light his pipe. He had to draw on it deeply several times before a red glow appeared in the bowl. "Unfortunately, we don't know how it works; we just know that it does."

"Good God, what kind of science is that?" asked Dad.

"I'm willing to try it," said Mom.

"My dear!" exclaimed Dad.

Mom bent over, rubbing her temples. "I'm sick to death of feeling low, Leo. I'm desperate to try anything that can help me get well."

After further discussion, Dr. Friedman drew up an admittance form, including permission to administer electroshock therapy. Mom signed the papers. Dad's signature wasn't necessary.

The following Monday, Dad cancelled his classes and I stayed home from school so we could move Mom into Woodbridge Sanatorium. We had a final family picnic lunch on the lawn. Dad had stopped at the deli and picked out all my favorites—fried chicken, potato salad, kosher dill pickles, and fruit cocktail—but I wasn't hungry. Mom tried to keep up a cheerful conversation, beginning several sentences with, "When I'm well…." The silences between our words grew longer.

I asked the question that had been gnawing at me for the past several days. "How long will you stay here, Mom?"

She smiled sadly, brushing the hair from my brow. "I don't know, Donna. I wish I did."

"A few days?" I suggested.

"Longer, I'm afraid."

"A week?"

Mom sighed and shook her head.

We gathered our picnic things, got mom's suitcase out of the car, and walked her to the admission office.

Dad stood before Mom, grasped her upper arms and pulled her face very close to his. "You can leave any time you want, Shirley. Any time of the day or night, just call me and I'll come get you. If you are dissatisfied in the very least…"

"I'll be fine, Leo. I believe in what Dr. Friedman has to offer me. I'm determined to get well."

"But if it proves to be too much for you…" Dad pleaded with his eyes.

My parents kissed so long, I had to look away. Mom's lashes were moist when she bent down to look into my face. "I'll be home as soon as I can, sweetie. You take good care of Daddy." She looked tired, but calm. She seemed relieved to be staying at Woodbridge.

As Dad and I walked to the parking lot, we passed a bench where three patients sat. One man stared vacantly as if he were blind, one woman rocked forward and backward, muttering about a jar with pebbles in it. The third person, a very old man with soft white whiskers billowing over his chest, seemed perfectly normal, except he smelled of poop.

Dad looked back at the large, imposing building where we had left Mom. I thought for a moment he was going to run back and carry her away in his arms. But he just shook his head and shuffled on. "The quack," he muttered through clenched teeth, more to himself than to me. "I hope he knows what the hell he's doing."

CHAPTER THIRTEEN

At home, Dad and I rattled around the house, too big for just the two of us. We filled it up with light and the sound of the TV. A housekeeper came in several times a week to do the heaving cleaning and laundry, but I did my best to set dinner on the table. At first it was only hot dogs, fish sticks, or frozen potpies, but then I started poking through Mom's cookbooks.

Dad's favorite salad was a gelatin, which he called "aspic," and I was determined to learn to make it. Mom had a dozen copper gelatin molds in various shapes—wreaths, hearts, fish, bumpy circles—displayed on the kitchen wall, and I selected the fish. I looked up her recipe for aspic, but the long list of ingredients seemed overwhelming. I couldn't just use Jell-O because the dish wasn't fruity or sweet. I had to use plain Knox gelatin by the tablespoon, along with tomato juice, chopped celery leaves, shredded cabbage, diced onion, crushed peppercorns, a sliver of garlic, and—worst of all—broth made from pigs feet. Where would I even find pigs feet? I decided to just use canned consommé instead.

After chopping and blending the ingredients, I dumped the mixture in the fish mold and placed it in the refrigerator. I worried that it wouldn't set and checked it every half hour. It seemed to be gelling fine. Just before dinner, I took my masterpiece out of the refrigerator and turned it over on Mom's special crystal plate. It wouldn't come out of the mold. I shook it. I prodded the side with a knife, which did nothing but gouged a big hole in the fish shape. I showed it to Dad who was reading the newspaper in his easy chair.

"Aspic, my favorite salad!" he exclaimed. "What a lot of trouble you've gone to, Donna girl."

"But I can't get it out of the mold."

"Try running a little warm water over it."

"O.K.!" I went back into the kitchen, turned the mold over on the plate, and placed it under the warm water faucet. Nothing happened. I made the water hotter. "Oh, oh!" I yelled.

"What is it?" Dad dashed to the kitchen and peered over my shoulder at the lumpy red glop running over the crystal plate. I was so disappointed I felt like crying.

"Gazpacho! My favorite soup!" exclaimed Dad.

I poured and scraped the mess into bowls. At dinner, he spooned his portion into his mouth, smacking his lips, but I couldn't force down more than a taste.

Mr. Goldfarb came over several times to help Dad prepare for his hearing before the House on Un-American Activities Committee. One evening I was in the kitchen washing the dishes while Dad and Mr. Goldfarb were meeting in the living room.

"They'll want to know why you opposed the hydrogen bomb," I overheard Mr. Goldfarb say.

"Again?" asked Dad. "Why don't they look it up in the file the CIA has on me. I'm sure it's all in there."

"Can you remember exactly what you told the Atomic Energy Commission at your last clearance hearing?"

"I don't remember word-for-word, Harry."

"If there's any discrepancy, they might try to trip you up, perhaps accuse you of perjury."

"It was my aim to reverse the arms race. Of course, the defense department resented it. You know they held Oppie, some of the others, and me responsible for the delay of the hydrogen bomb."

"I'm aware of that. And to this day they're convinced that a security leak enabled the Soviets to get the H-bomb much sooner than expected."

"I've never been accused of informing the enemy!" Dad said sharply. "That is not the issue here. Having my own ideas, allowing my students to think for themselves, that is the heart of the matter. All this hysteria over communism threatens our First Amendment rights."

Mr. Goldfarb sighed heavily. "You're preaching to the choir, Leo. Now, about your past, when you were still living in Austria. HUAC will grill you about that, too."

"In that case, they will get no answers."

"Leo, if you have something to hide, you must tell me about it."

"I have nothing at all to hide! My past is a personal matter. I will plead the Fifth."

"You could be held in contempt. Haven't you and your family been through enough without your getting hauled off to jail?"

"*Jail?*" I yelped. I dashed into the living room, drying my hands on a dishtowel.

"Look here, Harry. You're scaring Donna. There's no need to worry, Donna girl. Go back into the kitchen. You know it's rude to eavesdrop."

Dad and Mr. Goldfarb continued their conversation in hushed voices, so that I could no longer make out what was being said. The silences after Mr. Goldfarb's questions got longer, and after a while, I heard Dad wishing him good-night at the front door.

I went into the living room and sat quietly on the couch. Dad was at the bar, pouring himself a drink, not the fancy kind he made at cocktail parties, just scotch and a little water. He looked up and smiled wanly. "Shall we watch *Bonanza*, Donna?"

"No, thank you." My heart was pounding. When he sank into his easy chair with a grunt, I blurted, "Dad, I have a question. It's a grownup question."

His chin reared back and his eyes widened.

"Why did you leave your first wife, the one back in Austria?"

His heavy eyebrows bristled. "You may not ask me such things."

The heat rose to my face as if I had been slapped. He got up and turned on the TV. It was toward the end of the program, and the shoot out had already started. Little Joe shot a cowboy, and he spun around and fell dead in the dust. The Cartwrights killed one or more men every week, and it seemed to have no effect on them at all. Didn't they feel sorry or guilty? "Dad, why don't cowboys ever bleed?"

"To remind you it's not real."

"Couldn't you have taken her with you? Your first wife and…your son?"

"Oh, oh, such a long time ago." He rubbed his face so that his glasses rose up over his brow. "I have spent over twenty years trying to forget. Please don't ask me to remember now. My past has nothing to do with you."

"You're my father!"

The *Bonanza* theme began to play. I switched off the TV and returned to the sofa. I glared at my father, my arms crossed. He hauled himself out of his chair and poured himself another scotch and water. He poured 7-Up into a glass, added maraschino cherry juice, two cherries, and ice. He handed the drink to me, a compensation, I supposed, for not giving me what I wanted.

I clinked my glass against his. "Cheers."

His laugh was hollow. "Oh, good God, Donna. Cheers." He shuffled over to his chair and sank into it. We drank in silence. Finally he spoke. "If anyone ever tells you when you marry someone, you don't marry his family, don't believe it. I married into a Nazi family."

"Didn't you know that about them?"

"Yes, but I had had little experience with women. I had spent my entire life in classrooms and laboratories. I was foolish and naive and in love."

"What was she like?"

Dad lit a cigarette and blew smoke at the ceiling. "I didn't have time to get to know her. Courtship was very formal in Europe in those days. Men were expected to first establish themselves professionally, and then marry younger women. Gertrude was only seventeen when I was introduced to her at a ball. We met at such gatherings several more times, and then I asked her father for her hand in marriage."

"Why did you choose her?"

Dad tilted his head with a sigh. "I suppose I fell in love with my first wife for her hair of gold and my second wife for her heart of gold."

I smiled because Mom had blond hair, too. "What's your son's name?"

"It is of no importance now."

He's my brother, I wanted to remind him, but I changed the subject to keep him talking. "I didn't know there were Nazis in Austria."

"The Nazi party was very strong there. When Hitler invaded in 1938, it was not to conquer, but to lead the German-speaking people out of the Depression. Two hundred thousand Austrians rushed into the Vienna square to hail him as *Der Fuhrer*. It was on that day I became afraid."

"But you weren't Jewish."

"Many people were afraid of Hitler. He demanded absolute power, and people were expected to give up all personal freedom. I knew I would be forced to do his bidding, and I could not find it in my conscience to help him achieve the atom bomb."

"So you ran away. Did you ask your wife to come with you?"

"There was no chance of that. She believed everything her father told her. To speak against Hitler, to defect, was out of the question."

"Did you hope to be reunited later?"

"Sometimes you can't do things halfway, Donna. I knew I would never see my wife and son again. I did not expect to make it out of the country. I thought I'd be arrested and shot for treason."

I scooted to the edge of the sofa cushion, leaning toward him, hardly able to breathe for fear he would stop talking. "How did you escape?"

"When I was summoned to Berlin, I boarded the train in Vienna, but got off in Salzburg. From there, I crossed into Switzerland illegally, walking much of the way over the freezing Alps." He shifted his leg and pointed to it. "That's how I got this crippled knee. In London, I applied for passage to America, and ended up at Cal, working on the Manhattan Project."

"My history teacher said that was in New Mexico."

"Hundreds of people worked on the A-bomb, Donna. Our contribution at Cal was called electromagnetic separation."

"Oh. I'm sorry, Daddy. You had to go through so much."

He ground his cigarette in an ashtray. "It was a terrible war, Donna. Many people suffered far more than I. When I entered this country I was resigned to be solitary. I expected no personal happiness ever again, but Mommy insisted on it."

"Have you ever tried to contact…them?"

Dad looked at me, wide-eyed and resentful. "To say 'Hello, sorry to desert you?'"

I could tell it hurt him to speak of such things, but I kept pushing for answers. "What do you think happened to them?"

"Donna, please. How could I know? If they didn't die in the war, she remarried. He is a grown man. Many people died." Dad stared vacantly across the room, his fingers laced behind his head. I thought he was done talking, but then he continued. "I do know what happened to my father-in-law. It is public record. The reason he readily gave his Gertrude up to me, a poor scientist rather than an aristocrat, was because he was in disgrace. He had thrown a bomb into the shop of a Jewish jeweler, killing him. It was, of course, fine for a Nazi to kill a Jew, but he also kept the jewelry, distributing it among his family and mistresses." Dad's accent turned thick with bitterness. "He was stripped of his party honors, but reinstated later to run the death camp at Belzec. I can imagine how very satisfied he was, taking charge of murdering thousands of Jews and Poles. After the war, the British hunted him down, and while he was awaiting interrogation, he took cyanide."

I was shaken, certain I would have nightmares about death camps and suicide. "I'm sorry for giving you bad memories."

"Perhaps you are right, Donna. Perhaps you have prepared me for HUAC better than Harry."

I wanted to lighten up the subject before climbing the dark stairs alone. "Do you think Mommy will be O.K.?"

"I do. The rest cure is very effective. She'll have a good, long rest. Soon she'll return to us, Alice will come home, and we'll all be together as a family again."

"Dad, where's Alice?" I blurted.

He stared into his drink a long time, then glanced over at me as if he suddenly remembered I was in the room. "Isn't it your bedtime, Donna?"

I lost heart then. I could press him no more. I rose from the sofa, hugged him, and kissed his cheek. "Good-night, Daddy."

"Good-night, Donna." My foot was raised above the second stair, when he said softly, "Anton. His name is Anton."

A few days later, I entered the kitchen ready for school to find Dad, dressed in the suit he wore to the university, sitting at the table and staring into the backyard. I started his coffee percolating and fixed his bacon and scrambled eggs.

When I handed him his plate, he said, "I miss Mommy. Let's go see her today."

Mom had been at Woodbridge for a little over three weeks. We visited her on Sundays, but this was a Tuesday. "On a school day?" I sat across from him and poured cereal into a bowl.

Dad sipped his coffee and smacked his lips. "Why not on a school day? You should see how happy college students are when they read a cancellation post on a lecture hall door."

As we drove to Santa Rosa, Dad hardly said a word. I tried to make conversation, but after he said, "Pardon me?" several times, I gave up, thinking he must have something important on his mind.

At Woodbridge, we found Mom's private room vacant. Dad poked his head out of the room and addressed a nurse passing in the hall. "Where is my wife?" he asked, tension causing his voice to rise.

"I believe Mrs. Kronenberger is scheduled for therapy this morning."

"And where might that be?" The simple question came out more like an accusation.

The nurse looked hesitant. "I'll get Dr. Friedman for you."

Abruptly, a gurney rolled down the hall, pushed by two attendants and occupied by my mother who appeared to be asleep. We followed the gurney into her room, and the attendants shifted her onto the bed.

She stirred, her eyelids fluttering. She sat up, wincing in pain and pressing her fingertips against her skull. "Oh, my head." Her eyes widened when she noticed us in the room.

Dad rushed to her side and kissed her brow. "Darling, are you all right?"

She nodded. "Just a headache."

She looked at me. "What's your name?"

"Mommy, I'm Donna! Don't you recognize me?"

"Yes, of course, dear. I just forgot your book."

"Do you mean my name?"

Mom squinted at me and cocked her head. "Haven't you got a sister?"

"Yes, Alice."

"Where is she?"

"At your sister, Irene's," injected Dad, his face bunched with concern. "Don't you remember our arrangements, Shirley?"

"Oh, yes. Yes, I do." She held her palms against her temples. "I'm just a bit hazy. Things will clear up in a moment. Irene, Irene...is she the sister with the crippled girl?"

"Yes, dear, Gladys. She had polio," said Dad.

"Oh, that sister! Alice detests her! You're going to have to get her back right away. Alice is not happy there."

Dr. Friedman scurried into the room. The strands over the top of his head were mussed and he looked apprehensive. "Dr. Kronenberger, we didn't expect your visit today. If we had known you were coming, Mrs. Kronenberger's treatment would have been postponed."

"That's just what I want to discuss with you," said Dad, between a clenched jaw. "Mrs. Kronenberger's *treatment*."

Dad and Dr. Friedman stepped into the hall for a private conversation, but my father's voice bellowed so loudly, he could no doubt be heard all over the building. "Treatment, hell! My wife doesn't even know her own child!"

"Please calm yourself, Dr. Kronenberger," said the psychiatrist in a hushed, urgent tone. "The retrograde amnesia is merely temporary. She'll have her memory restored by your visit on Sunday."

Mom cocked her head at me. "Did you say you were Alice?"

"No, Mom, I'm Donna. My sister is Alice."

"She's the heavy set one, isn't she?" She leaned in closer to me and whispered, "Is she going to have a baby?"

It didn't seem fair to lie to somebody who was suffering from memory loss. "Yes, Mom," I admitted.

"I thought so. I forget her husband's name."

I raised my shoulders and dropped them. "She doesn't have a husband."

"Oh! Oh, I see." She pressed her curled forefinger against her upper lip. "Does your father know about this?"

"I think so."

We were silent a moment as Dad continued to rail again Dr. Friedman in the hallway.

Mom leaned toward me confidentially. "Perhaps it's best not to mention it to him."

The following Sunday during our visit to Woodbridge, Dad and I had lunch with Mom in the dining hall. She was wearing a flower-print dress and recently had had her hair done in a frosted, swirling poof. Her smile was sweet and the tension in her face muscles was relaxed, making her look years younger.

Dad gripped her hand across the table. "Darling, you look stunning!"

"I feel good." Mom added sugar to her iced tea and stirred. "This is a lovely place to take a rest, and the staff is so friendly."

"I'm so glad," said Dad. "What a state you were in Tuesday when we visited you. I gave Friedman a piece of my mind, I'll tell you."

Mom playfully rolled her eyes to meet Dad's. "I heard."

"What did he say to you?"

"No, I mean I heard you blowing your top out in the hallway. Really, Leo, there was no need."

Dad grinned sheepishly. "I apologized before we left. Didn't I, Donna?" He enthusiastically attacked his chop with his knife and fork. "I'm relieved those horrid electroshock treatments are behind you."

Mom added sugar to her ice tea and stirred. Did she realize she already had done it? "Leo, they're not."

"What? I gave Friedman explicit instructions to put a halt to them."

"And I told him to continue them."

"Shirley! Not really!"

"They're helping, Leo. I haven't felt this good in years, not in *years*."

"At what cost?" He pressed his palm to his chest. "To see how much you suffered wrenched my heart out."

"The shocks aren't painful, Leo, I assure you."

Dad's bushy brows rammed together. "I have a feeling you don't remember the pain. And we don't know how these treatments are affecting your brain. You heard Friedman admit that he doesn't know either."

"My brain is just fine." Mom took a bite of her potato and looked around the table. "Darling, will you pass me the salt and pumpkin?"

CHAPTER FOURTEEN

---•◦•---

The HUAC committee was scheduled to be in San Francisco, May twelfth through the fourteenth. Dad got the bad luck date: Friday, the thirteenth. By Wednesday of that week, I felt like jumping out of my skin. With Mom and Alice gone and me in school, who would be at the hearing to support Dad? I racked my brain trying to think what I could do about it. I decided I had to talk to Alice, no matter how big and pregnant and embarrassed she would be if I visited her.

I knew Mountain View was just down the peninsula, not far at all, and I could get there by train. I gathered up a handful of change and went down to the telephone booth on Vine and Shattuck. By making a couple of phone calls, I was able to check the train schedule and the visiting hours at the Samuelson Maternity Home.

Thursday morning, on my walk to school, I detoured down University Avenue and boarded the train for Mountain View. The ride was short, about an hour. When I got into the Mountain View station, I asked the conductor which bus to take to get to Maddox Street. I sat waiting for my bus and looking around for mountains to view. I didn't see any. The bus took me to a stop in front of a hospital, just across the street from the Samuelson Maternity Home. I walked into the foyer, my heart pounding. In a few minutes, I would see Alice! I had a feeling she wouldn't be too pleased about it.

The receptionist was working the switchboard, pulling plugs out of jacks and placing them in other jacks when the tiny lights above them blinked. For each call, she spoke into her headset, "Good morning, Samuelson Maternity Home. Extension, please." I waited a few minutes and when I didn't get her attention, I spoke in a loud, clear voice, "Excuse me, ma'am."

When she glanced over at me, I asked, "May I have the room number of Miss Alice Kronenberger, please?"

"May I ask who is visiting? Just a moment, please." She connected another call on her switchboard. "Good morning, Samuelson Maternity Home. Extension, please."

"Donna Kronenberger, her sister."

"You look rather young to be here by yourself. Don't you have school today? Just a moment, please." I waited some more, and then she said, "Do your parents know you're here? Just a moment, please. Good morning, Samuelson Maternity Home. Extension, please."

What if the receptionist didn't allow me to see Alice? Maybe I would have better luck with her if I found a pay phone and telephoned in. I could get Alice's room number, then sneak by her when she was busy at her switchboard. The next time I got her attention, I blurted, "My mother sent me on the train. She has an important message for Alice."

"Why didn't she come herself?"

"Oh, she can't. She's busy taking care of all our little brothers and sisters."

She narrowed her eyes at me. Several lights blinked on her board, and she connected more calls. I waited impatiently, shifting my weight from one foot to the other. What if she called our house to check on my story? No one would answer. What if she knew the number of my dad's office at the university? A tiny voice inside my brain tempted me to turn and bolt out the door.

Finally, the woman ran her red, pointed fingernail down a list at her elbow. "I'm sorry, Miss Kronenberger. Your sister isn't here."

"Yes, she is!" I sputtered. "I know for a fact she's here. I received a letter from her with this return address."

"She was here. Now's she's moved over there." She pointed across the street. I turned and looked, knowing I would see the hospital.

I dashed out of the building and across the street, asked for Alice's room number at the hospital reception counter, and without even waiting for the elevator, sprinted up the stairs to the maternity ward on the third floor. Breathlessly, I burst into Alice's room. The bed closer to the door had the curtain drawn around it, and someone was crying behind it. Propped up on the bed next to the window, sat Alice in a hospital gown, the covers drawn up to her armpits. She had visitors, three girls of various stages of pregnancy.

"Holy moly, Donna!" Alice exclaimed. "What are you doing here?"

"I need to talk to you. Are you going to have your baby soon?"

Alice glared back defiantly. "You got a screw loose? What baby?"

"This one!" I lunged at her blankets and pulled them down to her knees. I gasped at what I saw. Her belly was much too flat for a pregnant girl. "Alice! Where's your baby?"

Her three visitors burst into laughter. The red-haired and freckled one, who didn't look much older than me, rolled into the Mexican girl's lap. The Negro girl reared back and smacked her head against the wall. She was wearing a blue bandanna, which began to ooze blood.

"Oh, Lateesha! You've injured your poor head again," exclaimed Alice.

"Doesn't matter. I haven't had such a good laugh in a long time." She swiped off her headscarf, revealing a lumpy scalp. Circles of hair had been shaved, where scabs were closing over dime-sized sores. She gingerly pressed the cloth against the one that was bleeding.

I knew it was rude to stare, but I couldn't help myself. "What happened to you?"

"When her mama found out she was in a family way, she took off her shoe and beat her until the heel broke off," said the Mexican girl. "Then she kicked her out of the house."

"Don't you be telling the world my business," Lateesha scolded.

"I'm not the world. I'm Donna, Alice's sister."

"I'm Loretta," said the red-haired girl. "This is Yolanda and Lateesha." Loretta had a round face and wore a tiny gold cross. She was pale and very thin, except she looked like she had swallowed a beach ball. "I'll find you a chair."

She left the room. The person behind the curtain continued to sob in wails that rose and fell. Alice pressed her wrist to her brow and muttered through clenched teeth, "You think she could shut up a minute?"

"It's not easy," Yolanda said gently.

"We all feel the same way," snapped Alice. "A lot of good crying is going to do. You haven't had to listen to her for twelve hours straight."

Loretta returned to the room with a chair. "I had to sneak it," she said with an impish smile. "You know the rule: only three visitors at a time."

"Oh! Oh!" Yolanda clutched her middle. "He's doing summersaults in my stomach again."

"Not your stomach," said Lateesha. "You think he's some pork chop you had for dinner?"

"He's in your wound," said Loretta. "You know, how it says in the Hail Mary, 'Blessed is the fruit of thy wound, Jesus.'"

"Wound?" Lateesha pointed to her head. "Like these kind of wounds?"

Grinning, Alice cocked her head. "It's called a uterus."

"College girl knows the right names of things," said Lateesha.

Yolanda scrunched up her round, brown face. "Isn't uterus a planet?"

"That's Uranus," said Alice.

"Your anus?" exclaimed Lateesha. "That's a butthole!"

All the girls shrieked with laughter and rolled over each other again. A clicking of staccato heels caused a sudden silence.

"What's so funny?" A woman holding a clipboard of papers had entered the room. She wore a stiff, navy blue suit and a bun so tight her scalp looked like a peeled onion.

Alice looked at her with a solemn face, then snorted a laugh through her nose.

"I wouldn't think you girls would have much to laugh about." The woman looked me up and down, her steely gray eyes settling on my midriff. "Are you a new girl?"

"No, Mrs. Gregor," said Alice. "This is Donna, a *friend* from home. Donna, this is Mrs. Gregor, my social worker."

"I believe the whole point of your being here, Alice, is *not* to inform friends from home of your condition."

"What do you want?"

The woman sniffed at Alice's rude tone. "I'm here to see Patty. I'll attend to you later, after your company is gone."

"I thought we were done," Alice said warily.

"Well, we're not." Mrs. Gregor pulled opened the curtain surrounding the other bed. "Why did you request me, Patty? Everything's been arranged."

"I've changed my mind," exclaimed the weeping girl. "I want to keep my daughter."

"I'm afraid she's not yours to keep," said Mrs. Gregor. "You've relinquished the child to her adoptive parents. In return, as you are well aware, they are paying all your expenses, your room and board at Samuelson's and your medical bills here, which are quite substantial."

"I'll find some other way to pay. My mom said maybe my grandma can help."

"Now, Patricia, we've been over this. You well know if an unwed mother such as yourself takes on an illegitimate child, you and she will be ostracized from society forever. Do you really want an innocent child to suffer the brunt of your mistake?"

"No, but—"

"Of course, you don't." Mrs. Gregor handed the girl a Kleenex and patted her back. "You know what the child deserves: two legal parents, a mother and a father. Forget this ever happened and be a good girl from now on."

Patty's sobs were reduced to sodden gasps. Mrs. Gregor drew the curtains around her. We were all silent as she left the room.

"Witch!" Yolanda hissed. "Where's her broomstick?"

"She hates us," said Alice. "She thinks we're scum."

"She means well," said Loretta. "She knows what's best for our babies. Father Hugh told me an illegitimate baby can't be baptized. His poor little soul would end up in limbo. A married Catholic couple has to adopt him or he can never go to heaven."

"Are you going to hell for doing the nasty?" asked Lateesha.

Loretta face flushed magenta, clashing with her copper hair. "No, I went to confession. I told Father Hugh I had never heard of sexual intercourse, and it's the truth. The nuns never taught us any of that. My cousin, Joseph, just said he wanted to wrestle. I didn't know it could make a baby."

"Stupid-face Tony said I couldn't get pregnant the first time," said Yolanda. "He kept pressuring me to go all the way so I finally just gave in. It happened so fast I wasn't even sure we'd done it. Then he says, 'Now you're mine.' I didn't want to be *owned* by anybody, especially that jerk. I got rid of him as fast as I could, but then this came along." She patted the bulge in her middle. "His mama told me we had to get married. I said I wasn't getting married at no sixteen, and she says, 'You're selfish.' I think

I'm just the opposite. My baby is getting rich parents who can give him anything he wants."

"Well, I'm keeping my baby." Lateesha wrapped her arms around the slight bulge of her torso and rocked herself. "I don't care what!"

"You don't even got a place to stay for yourself." Yolanda waved her arm around the hospital room. "How are you gonna pay for all this?"

"I don't know, the lay-away plan, I guess."

Yolanda nodded toward Lateesha's belly. "What you think you got in there, *chica*, a washing machine?"

The girls whooped with laugher again.

Loretta rose to her feet awkwardly, pressing her hand into her lower back. "Well, I'm on KP for lunch today. I better go on across the street."

"I got laundry duty this week," said Lateesha. "Standing over a hot ironing board all afternoon until my legs swell up big as an elephant's."

The girls said their good-byes and left. "You should go, too, Donna," Alice said, looking toward the door as if she expected someone else.

"But I haven't even had a chance to talk to you."

Mrs. Gregor reentered the room. "Are you ready for me now, Alice? Oh, I see you still have company. I'll be back."

"What do you need?"

Mrs. Gregor glanced over at me, and then down at her clipboard. "I was going over the adoption papers. You've left the right side blank. It's imperative that you fill in the information about the father."

"I don't know a thing about him."

Mrs. Gregor stretched her mouth into a patient, fake smile. "Certainly you know his name."

Alice folded her arms and shook her head.

The social worker glanced over at me again, turned her back, and spoke to Alice in a low tone, as if that would prevent me from hearing her. "Am I to understand you're uncertain of the identity of the father?"

"Oh, right! You think we're all sluts!" Alice snapped. "There're lots of girls out there going all the way! We're just the ones who got caught!"

Mrs. Gregor reared back and tapped the paper with her pen. "About the father, now."

"There isn't one." Alice struggled to keep a straight face after such a ridiculous statement. "I did this all myself!"

"I'll come back when you're feeling a little more cooperative," said Mrs. Gregor.

I waited until I could no longer hear her retreating footsteps before I leaned confidentially toward Alice to ask her a question she might refuse to answer. "Does Kenneth know?"

"What would he care?" She pointed across the street, in the direction of the maternity house. "I had plenty of time to sit around that joint thinking things over. Kenneth didn't care about me, he didn't care about Angela, he doesn't give a damn about anybody except maybe his pals."

"He took advantage of you."

"Oh, please, Donna, where did you pick up such an expression? I knew having sexual intercourse could lead to pregnancy, I just didn't believe it could happen to me. I wanted to run wild, I ran wild. I wanted to be cool. Look how cool I am!" She shook her finger at me. "Don't ever blame the boy, Donna, unless it's rape. We girls have to learn to look out for ourselves."

A nurse in a white uniform and winged cap entered the room, a black furry ball appearing above her forearm. "Feeding time, Miss Kronenberger," she announced.

"Your baby!" I exclaimed. "Oh, Alice, your baby!"

"You need to go, Donna. Right now!" She pointed to the door. "Good-bye!"

"Oh, but I want to see him. Or is it a her?"

The nurse placed the tiny, red wrinkly-faced baby into Alice's arms. "Here he is." She handed her a bottle and withdrew.

"It's a he!" I clapped my hands and bounced in my chair. "Oh, Alice, you have a son!"

"No, I don't. I'm just the one who gave birth to him." She nudged the nipple of the bottle between his lips, and the baby sucked greedily. "Three days! That's all I get with him, and then I have to forget he exists. How am I supposed to forget him now that you've seen him? We can't both forget. Damn it, Donna, you're not supposed to be here!"

I scooted my chair forward to get a better look. "Oh, he's precious! Isn't there some way you could—"

"You know there isn't. Our parents would die of mortification if I brought him home. I'd have no money to raise him, no chance to go back to college, and no one would ever want to marry me."

"He has Dad's nose! Does Dad know you're...?"

"Of course, he knows-knows, but he doesn't know. Dig?"

"I think so. I tried to get him to admit it once."

"Oh, Donna, you shouldn't have. Dad is very old country. He'll never say a word about this as long as he lives." The baby squirmed and shifted, cuddling closer to Alice. "Ah," she said, smiling down on him. "Aren't you the sweetest thing?"

"You won't ever get to see him again? Not ever?"

"No. The adoptive parents won't know me, and I won't know them. When he's eighteen, he'll be allowed to check his file at Vital Statistics, but most kids never want to meet the parents who deserted them. Some of them feel it's disloyal to their adoptive parents. Donna, don't you dare tell anyone you saw him! Not Dad, not Mom, not Mary Lou, no one."

"I'm not that good of friends with Mary Lou anymore." I was itching to tell someone though. I thought of Randy, but if Mrs. Greene got wind of it, she'd go up and down our street dragging our whole family in the mud.

"How'd you get here anyway?" asked Alice.

"Train."

"Do Mom or Dad knew what you're up to?"

I shook my head. "Nobody does."

"Thank God. My reputation is ruined, but we can't let this destroy your life, too. People think if one girl in a family is loose, the sister will be, too."

"I don't care what people think! Don't Mom and Dad get to see their grandchild?"

"Don't call him that! He doesn't belong to us. How are the keepers, anyway? Is Mom still in the nut house?"

"She's still a patient at Woodbridge. She's trying hard to get better. She's having electroshock therapy."

"Cripes, sounds like a science fiction movie!"

"She says it's helping. Dad is having fits about it."

"Poor, fragile Mommy. She was wonderful to me. I was a basket case when I found out I was expecting and she took care of everything, paid for it, too, not like the parents of a lot of these girls. She never scolded me or blamed me. She said this happens to a lot of girls, but it's all kept secret.

She took care of Dad, too, in her own demure way, protecting him from my girl trouble. How is Dad, by the way?"

"That's what I came to talk to you about. He goes before HUAC tomorrow. He's got to face them all alone."

"What happened to Mr. Goldfarb?"

"I mean us—Dad's family."

Alice raised an eyebrow at me. "Donna, don't get any ideas. The most help you can give Dad is to stay away."

"But Mr. Goldfarb says he could go to jail!"

Alice shook her head. "It isn't likely. They just want to scare him, humiliate him, because pompous J. Edgar Hoover thinks he insulted the FBI with his innocent little quiz question. You're not to mettle, Donna, like you're doing here. You saw a baby that isn't suppose to exist!"

"I'm glad I did! I'm his auntie! I'm never going to forget him! I'll think of him breathing and happy and growing up in the world somewhere." I thought of Anton then. I imagined two babies floating around the earth, hand-in-hand. Then I remembered our half brother was a grown man.

Alice smiled down at her baby. "Let's have a real look at you." Resting him against her thighs, she unwrapped his blanket. There he was, rosy and perfect. Ten little fingers and ten little toes. The baby stretched and began to suck again as if the bottle were still in his mouth, causing us both to laugh. Alice unpinned his diaper. "Just look at this little man!" she exclaimed. "I'm glad he's a boy. I'm glad he'll never have to grow up and suffer like a girl!"

The nurse strode efficiently in the room and skidded to a halt. "My word, what are you doing to that baby?"

"Just looking at him," Alice said sheepishly, fumbling with the diaper.

"He's not a doll! Don't you know he'll catch his death of cold?" scolded the nurse.

"I thought it was warm enough in here," Alice muttered, her chin against her throat.

"You haven't any idea what you're doing. It looks like I got here just in time." The nurse hastily wrapped the baby, scooped him up, and whisked him out of the room.

"Wait! I..." Alice stretched her empty arms toward her baby, then let them drop limply at her sides.

CHAPTER FIFTEEN

That same afternoon, I was back home, twirling batons in my backyard with Randy, just like it was any normal school day. He had decided he liked twirling so much, he had bought his own baton.

I tossed my baton with all my might. Looking for it high in the sky, I saw Alice's little naked baby boy squirming among the tree branches. The baton hurled down through the glaring light and conked Randy on the head. "Ow! You're sure a klutz today, Donna."

"Gee-whiz, Randy. Sorry. I guess I got a lot on my mind."

"I guess you do! I read in the paper your dad goes before HUAC tomorrow."

"Uh-huh." I hadn't thought of going to the hearing until Alice had given me the idea. "If I found a way to get to San Francisco, do you think they'd let me into the hearing?"

"They'd have to. It's public."

"Then I got a super huge favor to ask you. Would you drive me to San Francisco tomorrow?"

Randy scrunched his face, looking like he was going to say no. "Can't you go with your dad?"

"He'd say no, then forbid me to go. I have to find a way to sneak in. You think I can get in the room without him noticing?"

He Nodded. "It will probably be big and crowded, but what's the point of that?"

"He needs me there, even if he doesn't realize it."

"He'll realize nothing if you're going to hide from him."

"Just at first, and then…oh, I don't know what then. Just forget it! I'll figure out which bus to take."

"Hold it. Let me think." Randy rubbed his cheek with the ball of his baton. "We'd have to make up some excuse to take my mom's car to school."

"You mean you'll do it?" I threw my baton and caught it behind my back with a twirl. "That's just terrif! I've never been in the city by myself. I'd be petrified."

"I wouldn't be able to stay. I'd have to leave you there and go straight back to school."

"You would? How come?"

"Are you kidding? The attendance secretary would call my house, and my mom would have the highway patrol sending out an all-points bulletin. Are you sure you want to go through with this?"

I bit my lip and nodded.

"All right. Let's think up some song and dance to tell my mom."

We twirled and thought until Randy came up with the idea of bringing the gigantic medieval castle he had made in sixth grade to our sophomore world history class for extra credit. Only Mrs. Greene would believe we still studied castles in high school.

"Good plan," I said. "Hey, have you ever driven into the city?"

He shot me his toothy Chinaman leer. "Confucius say: there's a first time for everything."

"Oh, brother!" I smiled back weakly, thinking of car crashes, traffic tickets, and accidentally driving off the Bay Bridge, but he had to be a better driver than Alice.

The next morning, Mr. Goldfarb arrived early to our house to drive Dad to the HUAC hearing. They both looked stiff and unsure in their dark suits. I hugged my dad and he patted my head.

"Now, Donna, you're not to worry. I'll be home for dinner, I promise."

"O.K., Dad."

"If any cranks telephone, just hang up. If the press calls with any questions, just say 'No comment,' to anything they ask."

"I will. Good luck."

Mr. Goldfarb shook my hand and produced a quarter from my sleeve. "How about that? Money for ice cream on your way home from school."

"Thank you, Mr. Goldfarb."

"I had nothing to do with it. That money came from your magic sleeve."

As soon as they left, I dashed over to Randy's. He met me at the back door. "Come on into my room and give me a hand with the castle."

We tried to pass through the pink kitchen, wallpapered with a China doll print, but Mrs. Greene blocked our way. She was in a quilted robe with bits of hair sticking out of pink foam curlers. "Finish you Cream of Wheat, Randy."

"Aw, Mom. We gotta go."

She pointed at the table. "Sit. The both of you. Donna can wait for you to finish your breakfast. How's your sister, Donna? I haven't seen her in ages."

"She's fine."

"Where has she gone off to?" Mrs. Greene smiled so wide I could see her pointy teeth.

"She's in Oregon, visiting our Aunt Irene."

"My, such a long, long visit. Dropped out of college, has she? I always say no need for a girl to go to college except for her M-R-S, if you know what I mean. And your mother—I haven't seen her in a long while either. How's she doing?"

"Fine."

Mrs. Greene reared back her head. "Really? Then I can squash some nasty gossip that Marge Brighton is spreading around the neighborhood. She says your father had your mother committed."

"Mom," said Randy.

"Let Donna have her say."

My cheeks burned, but I held my head high. "My mother has gone for a rest at a nervous hospital. It's just for a few weeks."

Mrs. Greene tapped her fingernails on the tabletop. "Well, I suppose I'd be nervous, too, if I was married to a communist."

I didn't even try to defend Dad against Mrs. Greene. She had her own ideas about the way things were, and I certainly wasn't going to change them.

Randy shoved his bowl aside and leaped from his chair. In the hallway, he muttered, "Sorry about my mom and her nosey questions."

"It's O.K."

"It's an embarrassment! Just be glad your dad is going up against HUAC instead of her."

I hadn't been in Randy's bedroom since I was eight. His bedspread still depicted the Lone Ranger, and his coonskin cap topped a bedpost. On a long counter were every school, Boy Scout, and Erector project he'd ever made, his Wham-o boomerang, chemistry set, and Pez dispenser collection lovingly displayed and dusted by Mrs. Greene. I picked up his ant farm and gave it a shake, but all I could see was dirt.

"They died," said Randy.

Together we carried his old castle, with the toilet-paper-roll turrets coming unglued, down the hall and into the back seat of his mom's car.

"Don't forget your sweater, Randy," Mrs. Greene called from the back porch, but he was already backing the big sedan out of the garage and pretended not to hear her.

I should not have worried about an accident, because once we got onto the bridge, the stop-and-go commuter traffic across the bay and down Market Street moved at a snail's pace. A traffic jam made it impossible to turn on Polk Street. Hundreds of people carrying signs were crowded into Civic Center Plaza across the street from City Hall.

"What's going on?" I asked.

"I dunno," said Randy. "Maybe some Civil Rights demonstration, like that one they had a little while ago trying to get the hotels and restaurants to hire Negroes."

"It doesn't look like we can go any farther. I'll just bail out here."

Randy clutched my arm. "Wait, it doesn't look safe. These demonstrations sometimes get violent. Are you positive you wanna go through with this?"

"Since when do you think I turned chicken?"

Randy squinted and tilted his head, trying to get a better view of the gathering. "Well, O.K. A lot of Cal students participate in these things. One of them can tell you what bus to take back to Berkeley."

I tried to slide out of the car, but Randy clung to the sleeve of my sweater. "Be careful."

I pried Randy's hand off me and gave it a squeeze. "Thanks for the ride." Maybe a girl and a boy could be good friends.

Walking down Polk Street, I was able to read the signs of the protesters, parading in an oblong formation before City Hall.

"We walk to preserve freedom."

"Defend the Bill of Rights."

"The Un-American Activities Committee is Anti-American."

I had heard this reasoning in my own home, but was amazed to see so many people who thought the same way. Dad wasn't alone! All these people were on his side.

TV news broadcasters were recording the event. A cluster of reporters pressed microphones into the face of a distinguished-looking man. I moved in closer to hear what he was saying.

One newsman asked, "Congressman Willis, can you explain why the HUAC hearing is being held?"

"With respect to the general operation of the communist conspiracy wherever it may lead. It's a mandate. The law has been on the books for probably twenty years."

"Are all these people communists?" asked the newscaster.

"I can answer that," said a man who accompanied the Congressman. "These are mostly students from the University of California and San Francisco State College. They're ordinary kids like yours and mine, except that they're activated by trained communist agitators and propagandists."

I scanned the area for communist agitators, not really knowing what they would look like. Did they wear trench coats and sunglasses and talk in Russian accents? I didn't find anybody like that.

City Hall was enormous, covering two whole blocks. Mounting the steps, I wondered how I would ever find the room where Dad's hearing would be held. I joined the crowd of people shuffling into the rotunda and craned my neck to gaze up at the wide dome arcing high above me. Everything in the room looked rich and fancy: the statues, medallions, and lighting fixtures, the ornate marble floor, and the sweeping grand staircase with curlicue bronze handrails.

"Oh!" I gasped. "Oh!"

"Like crazy gorgeous, huh?" said a coed wearing a peasant dress and resting a "Ban the Blacklist" picket on her shoulder. "The dome is higher than our nation's capital. Marilyn Monroe got married there on that staircase, right at the top."

"She did? Well, it's beautiful," I replied, happy that the girl was so chatty and friendly.

"Right-o, but this crowd is about ready to tear it down."

"Oh, do you really think so?"

"Naw, a few scuff marks on this pink marble floor maybe. Don't worry, kiddo. They've got plenty of peons to get down on their hands and knees and shine it all up again."

"Do you know where the HUAC hearing is?"

She nodded toward the staircase. "Up there and down the hall. Good luck getting in."

I made my way slowly up the stairs and pushed through the people in the hall.

"Hey, no cuts," someone yelled at me.

"Sorry," I said. "I'll go back to the end of the line. I just want to see in." When I reached the door of the hearing room, I stood on tiptoe, trying to get a glimpse through the octagonal window.

A policeman blocked my view, holding his billy club lengthwise before my throat. "Step back! Step back!" he ordered.

Two men in suits and a lady in a mink stole, gloves, and veiled hat passed all the students waiting in line. The lady showed the policeman a white paper, and he let her and her companions into the room. The students booed.

"No fair," shouted someone.

"I've been waiting my turn to get in since yesterday afternoon," said another.

The policeman ignored them, continuing to stare straight ahead.

I turned to a co-ed leaning against the wall, eating dried figs out of a wax paper sandwich bag. "What did that lady show him?"

"A pass."

"How do you get one of those?"

She chewed thoughtfully. "No one knows. It appears that only the people who are sympathetic to HUAC are allowed in."

"But they gotta let me in. My dad has been subpoenaed to appear before the committee today."

She cocked her head with interest. "Who's your dad?"

"Dr. Leopold Kronenberger," I said proudly. "He's a physics professor at Cal."

"Oh, yeah, I read about him in the *Daily Californian*. Maybe he can get you a pass."

"Maybe," I muttered, if only I could admit to him I was here. I wandered back to the end of the line, stepping over the legs of people who sat against the wall. I stood so long that the back of my knees ached. A few other grownups with passes walked by and were ushered into the room, but none of the students.

"You can't keep us out," yelled a boy in a Cal sweater. "We have a Constitutional right to be in there."

I wondered what the committee members were asking Dad. Was he giving them the answers they wanted to hear or was he going to be arrested? The suspense gave me a queasy stomach. I made my way downstairs and outside to get some fresh air. A large, wide column of people was marching down Polk Street.

I overheard people around me talking about it. There had been an American Civil Liberties rally against HUAC in Union Square that morning, and now the participants were marching over to City Hall and assembling in the plaza. More policemen, many of them old and out-of-shape, arrived in paddy wagons. They were dressed in helmets, boots, and combat gear. I wondered who they planned to battle. There were lots of people, but everyone looked peaceful and law-abiding.

The wind blew cold, and I only had on a sweater. I followed some of the Civil Liberties marchers into City Hall. This time it was harder to squeeze between the people jammed into the rotunda. I used the handrail to pull myself up the stairs and then I pushed through the crowded hallway toward the hearing room.

Suddenly a demonstration within the hearing room broke out. People were chanting, "Open the door! Open the door! Open the door or get out of town!" They burst into singing "The Star-Spangled Banner" and we in the hallway joined in.

The doors flew open. Two policemen held the arms of a man walking between them.

"Ah, an uncooperative witness," commented a young man next to me. "Off to jail he must go."

The witness tried to wriggle free. "I can walk outta here myself," he grumbled.

The hearing recessed for lunch. Observers filed out of the room. I ducked behind some students, but I didn't see Dad or Mr. Goldfarb. I found out later that the Congressmen, the witnesses, and their lawyers exited and entered from a door not accessible to the public.

My stomach growled, but I hadn't thought how I would eat lunch. I only had enough money for the bus. If I just sat in the hall outside the empty hearing room during the lunch break, maybe I would have a better chance of getting into the next session. Other people had the same idea. There were rumors floating about that more observers would be allowed into the afternoon hearing.

The rumors were false. Just like the morning, only older people all dressed up and showing passes were allowed in. The students in the hall and the rotunda began to sing protest songs and clap, the sound reverberating in the spacious dome. Policemen came rushing into the building and up the stairs. They began to unwind the fire hoses. I wondered why. There was no fire alarm and no smoke. Were they checking the equipment? Wouldn't that be the job of firemen?

One policeman shouted, "So you want some of this? Well, you're going to get it."

The blast came with no other warning. Suddenly people began stumbling, falling, and sliding down the grand staircase as if an unseen force pushed them. The force was actually water blasting from the fire hoses, washing people down the stairs and flushing them out of the rotunda. Some people walked peacefully to the exit, while others passively resisted by sitting down on the steps. Policemen grabbed them by their clothing, arms, or legs and pushed or carried them down the stairs and outside to the waiting paddy wagons.

Before I could recover from the shock of what I was witnessing, I felt the blast of cold, stinging needles from behind. The powerful spray knocked my legs out from under me, and I was bouncing down the slippery marble stairs—*boom, boom, boom*—on each step my bottom feeling jarred and bruised. I flung an arm around the railing and hung on, but a policeman tried to pull my hands away. Was he going to arrest me? For what? I couldn't get arrested; I wasn't even supposed to be here! I kicked and screamed, "Get off me, get off! I haven't done anything!"

The policeman succeeded in prying my hands free, and with a mighty grunt, hurled me down the stairs. I felt my head bouncing against the railing as I slid out of control, faster, faster, too fast to grab on to anything. The last few stairs curved out before me—so beautiful, like a pink wedding cake. I felt a crushing pain explode in my head, and then everything went black.

CHAPTER SIXTEEN

I became aware of metal clinking in the distance, silverware maybe, my mom getting dinner. My head pounded. I opened my eyes to narrow slits, screened by my lashes. I was in a hospital bed! Why would I...? Oh, yeah, the HUAC hearings, the water from the fire hose forcing me down the staircase. I opened my eyes wider. *Ow*, my head! The curtain around the patient next to me was closed and from behind it I heard faint snoring. No one else was in the room. Didn't they allow Dad to sit with me? There were probably strict visiting hours, which was just as well. I knew I was really in dutch for going to the city without his permission.

I had to go to the bathroom, but it was painful to move. If I didn't force myself to get up, I would wet the bed. Slowly, I swished one leg, then the other, over the edge of the mattress. I sat up. *Bam, bam* went the pulse in my head. I felt faint. I remembered I hadn't eaten since breakfast. Was it still Friday? The soft lighting in the room indicated it was night. I waited for the wooziness to pass, then slid carefully down until my feet touched the cold floor.

I walked holding onto the bed, then a chair, and then the doorway of the bathroom. I swung the door shut, but it didn't latch. I was wearing only a hospital gown opened in the back, which made it easy to plop down on the toilet. After peeing, I sat there a moment, trying to gain the strength to stand.

Through the cracked door, I heard someone enter the room and exclaim, "Jane Doe is missing!"

What a funny name. I'd heard of John Doe, meaning someone who couldn't be identified. Holding onto the sink, I pulled myself up. In the mirror, I saw that I had a bandage around my head. I pressed my fingertips lightly over the gauze, checking for damage. *Ow!* There it was, over my right ear, a large goose egg, where I must have hit the bronze railing. I shuffled out of the bathroom to find two nurses standing over my empty bed.

"Oh, there you are," said one nurse with orange hair and big hips.

"Is my dad here?"

"Who's your dad?" she asked.

"More to the point, who are you?" asked the second nurse, who was little and brown, maybe Filipino. "Do you remember your name?"

So I was Jane Doe! "Um, yeah. Donna. Donna Kronenberger."

"Well, hello, Donna. How are you?" asked the big nurse.

"I'm hungry."

"That's a good sign."

"And my head hurts."

"That's no surprise," said the Filipino nurse. "I'll ask doctor if you are allowed to eat something." She left the room.

"Do you remember where you live?" asked the other nurse.

"Berkeley."

"In the dorms?"

That made me smile, which hurt my head. "No. I live with my family."

"Do you remember your phone number?"

"I remember everything up until the time I hit my head," I said. She gave me a hefty boost into bed, and I told her my phone number. "What day is it?"

"Still Friday," she said, checking a watch that was pinned to her bosom. "A little before eight. You've been out several hours."

"Where am I?"

"San Francisco General. I'll call your parents. I'm sure they've been worried sick about you. Did they know you were at City Hall?"

"Um…no."

The nurse clicked her tongue. "That explains why you haven't been identified yet. You look pretty young to be attending a riot on your own."

"A riot?"

She handed me a stack of rumpled newspapers from off a visitor's chair. "Here, you can read all about it."

The headline of the *San Francisco Examiner* read "486 Students Arrested outside HUAC Hearings." There was a huge photo of people being hosed down the staircase of the rotunda. The article said that eight students had been hospitalized and eight police officers as well, mainly for exhaustion. Below that story was a smaller article with the title "Red Probe Still Scheduled Tomorrow Despite Protests."

I was given pain medicine and my dinner, which wasn't bad at all—chicken, green beans, fake mashed potatoes, and a little paper cup of ice cream. I felt much better by the time Dad walked into the room. I knew he wasn't too angry with me because he had stopped at the gift shop for a Snickers and the latest *Sixteen*.

"Donna girl! How's your dear head?" Dad lightly grazed his fingertips over my ear.

"It's just a little bump. I'm sorry for going into the city without your permission."

"You shouldn't have done it. I've been out of my wits looking for you. I called Mommy and she gave me the names of every friend of yours she could think of. I must have made a dozen calls."

"Didn't Randy tell you where I was?"

"Randy?" Dad's brow creased. "Randy next door?"

"He drove me," I admitted. "Oh, please don't yell at him, Dad. I talked him into it. It's all my fault! And don't tell Mrs. Greene! She doesn't know he drove her car into the city, and, well, you know how she is."

He nodded solemnly. "I do, indeed."

"What a mad house, Dad! Did you hear the police turning the fire hoses on us?"

"We heard a commotion outside the hearing room, but we had no idea what was taking place. When the session was abruptly adjourned, we were astounded to discover janitors sweeping water out of the rotunda. I assumed a water main had burst. Then Harry stopped to talk to a gentleman outside the building who told him when the demonstrators refused to leave, the police threatened them with the hose."

"That's not how it happened! The police didn't warn us at all!"

"No order to disburse over a bullhorn? Maybe you didn't hear it."

"I was right there! The hose were a surprise attack! All that water flooding the inside of that beautiful building! Weren't they worried about water damage?"

"Apparently not. Nor people damage, for that matter. You're fortunate you weren't seriously hurt, Donna. Whatever possessed you to attend a demonstration?"

"I didn't know I was going to a demonstration! I thought I was going to the HUAC hearing. They wouldn't let any of us in, and I couldn't stand it that you were in there all alone."

"I was hardly alone, Donna."

"You know what I mean. Without Mom, without any of us. How'd it go anyway? Did they let you off?"

Dad sighed and rubbed his broad hand over the top of his head. "They didn't get through as many subpoenaed witnesses that they had scheduled. I have to return tomorrow."

"Oh! Can I go with you?"

He pinched his thick upper lip, thinking. "I'm not sure that's best for you."

"Please! Can Mr. Goldfarb get me a pass? That was the whole problem today, you know. They weren't letting the students into the hearing. You had to have a pass."

"I supposed the committee was worried about interference. They got that, all right."

"Please, Dad! I'll sit quietly. You won't hear a peep out of me, I promise."

"I'm not worried about your behavior, sweetie. It's the committee's. I'm not certain the questions they will ask me are fit for your ears."

"But you already told me about your past in Austria, and I know you didn't want to work on the H-bomb. What else could they ask?"

"I don't know, Donna. I just don't want to subject you to it."

"I can take it! I'm not afraid of HUAC or rotten old J. Edgar Hoover or the police or anybody. You might need—what's that kind of courage other people give you?"

"Are you speaking of moral support?"

"That's it." I reached for his hands and squeezed them tightly. "I can give you moral support!"

Dad's smile was very strange. It looked like he was going to cry. He swallowed hard and said, "We'll have to see what your doctor says."

We talked a little longer. He said that Mom was feeling much stronger and would be returning home soon. I wanted badly to tell him I had visited Alice, but I knew for his sake I had to go on pretending she was at Aunt Irene's. Did he know she had had her baby? Someone at Samuelson's Maternity Home must have contacted him. Didn't he want to see his grandchild? No, the baby wasn't his grandchild, not even a member of our family. He belonged to his adoptive parents now.

The doctor came in to examine me. He was a short, older man with creases down his face and droopy eyelids. He introduced himself as Dr. Bauer. "So you are Donna, are you?" He spoke with a German accent like Dad's.

"Yes. Can I go home now?"

"Not so fast, Miss Donna. You have quite a lump on the noggin. I will have to keep you overnight for observation."

"Then can I go? Tomorrow morning? Early tomorrow morning?"

"We shall see." He listened to my heart with his stethoscope, and then without another word, shuffled out of the room.

"That man needs some sleep," said Dad.

"You noticed, too? Please, let me go to the hearing with you tomorrow."

"I'll see what Harry has to say about it."

"He'll say yes, I know he will. I'll need some dress-up clothes. Can you bring them to me tomorrow?" I told him which dress, shoes, hat, and gloves to pack. I also had to say I needed a slip, bra, under panties, nylon stockings, and a garter belt, which embarrassed the both of us. "Look in my top dresser drawer. If you can't find the garter belt there, look under my bed."

Dad's eyebrows rammed together. "What's it doing thee?"

"I get mad at it sometimes," I admitted.

That night I hardly got any sleep. Whenever I dozed off, a nurse would come around, pry open my eyes, and shine a little flashlight into my pupils. After the third time, I got pretty fed up, but I knew I had to be a cooperative patient to be released.

In the morning, a nurse I hadn't seen before gave me a sponge bath in my bed and unwrapped my bandage. I had breakfast and waited and waited for Dr. Bauer, who finally came in to look at my head.

"I'm going to release you from the hospital, but you be careful, young lady." He shook his finger at me. "Don't go climbing any trees just yet."

I was about to tell him I hadn't climbed a tree since I was little, but then I remembered I did have to get my baton if it got stuck in the branches. "I won't," I promised.

A nurse wrapped my head in a fresh bandage, and then I waited some more for Dad. Just when I started to get worried that he had gone to the hearing without me, he arrived with my things in Mommy's overnight case. He left the room to give me a chance to change. He didn't know to bring the dress on a hanger, and I tried my best to smooth out the wrinkles it got from being all smashed up. At the front desk downstairs, I was discharged from the hospital. We met Mr. Goldfarb in the waiting room. He reached behind my ear and produced a golf ball.

I had to laugh, touching my head. "There's still one in there!"

"I like your headband, Donna. It just might help your dad's case."

"Damn it, Harry, we are *not* going to exploit my child." Dad took my wide-brimmed hat from my hand and placed it on my head. When he started out the revolving door, Mr. Goldfarb pushed my hat farther back to reveal a glimpse of the bandage.

CHAPTER SEVENTEEN

During the drive over to City Hall, Mr. Goldfarb advised Dad. "Just answer the questions, Leo. You have nothing to hide. Willis and his committee will see that you're being straightforward. They'll let you off, and we can all go home and forget this HUAC nonsense."

"You're right, Harry. I'll cooperate, for my family's sake. I'm just as eager to put all this fiasco behind me."

Since it was a Saturday, traffic was light throughout San Francisco. The closer we got to City Hall, however, the more congested it was. There were even more demonstrators gathered in the plaza than the previous day. Some of the protesters extended their arms in a "Heil, Hitler" motion. The slogans on their pickets read

"Uphold the First Amendment."

"Down with the Police State in America."

"Fascism is not our national policy yet."

We walked around the building to a side door, guarded by a policeman. Mr. Goldfarb showed him a pass, and we were allowed inside. We took seats in the gallery of the hearing room, while we waited for Dad to be summoned to the bar. The HUAC committee members filed in and took their seats at a long table at the front of the room. Congressman Willis first summoned Archie Brown.

"Here we go again," muttered Mr. Goldfarb.

"Isn't this the third time for him?" whispered Dad.

"It's all for show," said Mr. Goldfarb. "HUAC and uncooperative witnesses are in competition to gain the sympathies of the media. The committee repeatedly calls up uncooperative witnesses to make it look like they have something to hide, as the witnesses try to demonstrate they are being persecuted. Nothing but a circus act."

"Where are the elephants?" I asked him.

He grinned at me and pushed my hat back to show my bandage. Dad gave him a stern look and slid it forward again.

Once Archie Brown and his lawyer were seated at the witness table, the committee began to ask him questions. "What is your occupation?"

"Longshoreman. I have something to tell the committee—"

"Where were you born?"

"Iowa. I want to tell the committee my family is being threatened—"

"The witness has been ordered and directed to answer the question. Are you represented by counsel?"

"Yes."

"Counsel, would you identify yourself?"

His lawyer leaned toward the microphone and said his name.

Mr. Brown said, "I have something—"

"I repeat," said Congressman Willis. "Answer the question. That is the only way we can proceed orderly."

"What was the question?" asked Mr. Brown.

Observers in the hearing room murmured and tittered.

"Where were you born?"

"I already answered that. I want to read this statement."

"You may file your statement; you may not read it."

Each time Mr. Brown was asked a question, he tried to read a sentence of his statement. Finally two policemen lifted him out of his seat by his arms and escorted him out of the hearing room.

Another witness who was summoned was William Mandel. He was an arrogant-looking man, with black hair and sunglasses.

A male voice behind me said, "An identified agent of the Communist party."

Another observer whispered, "A Sovietologist."

"Kicked out of Stanford University's Hoover Institute because he's a commie," someone else declared.

As soon as Mr. Mandel was seated in the witness chair, the HUAC committee began to interrogate him. Mr. Mandel burst out, "If you think that I am going to cooperate with this collection of Judases, of men who sit there in violation of the United Sates Constitution, if you think I'll cooperate with you in any way, you are insane!"

Thunderous applause broke out, and then Mr. Mandel was also escorted out of the room. When the excitement died down, Congressman Willis called, "Dr. Leopold Kronenberger."

I grabbed Dad's hand and squeezed it. He had promised to answer the questions, and after dealing with Mr. Brown and Mr. Mandel, the committee would be so relieved to have a cooperative witness that they were sure to dismiss him.

Dad and Mr. Goldfarb moved to the witness table. From where I was seated I could only see his profile. The Congressmen interrogated him for over an hour. Their questions were about his past life in Vienna, his coming to the United States, and his work and teaching here. Sometimes a question made Dad's face flush with indignation, and he had to swallow hard before speaking, but he gave an answer. He was cooperating. Eventually Congressman Willis asked him the question the committee asked every witness.

"Are you now or have you ever been a member of the Communist party?"

"No."

"Are you sympathetic to communism?"

"It is not against the law in this country to belong to the Communist party."

"Just answer the question, Dr. Kronenberger."

"It is not a simple question. Are you asking if I share any ideology of the Communist party? I do. I believe all people have the right to earn a fair wage and enjoy a decent standard of living, same as the communists."

"Were you sympathetic to the Soviets when you decided not to work on the hydrogen bomb?"

"I was not. I do not believe genocide is an acceptable defense strategy. I therefore advised against developing the super. I once lived in a country where scientists were forced to bend to political policy and to have a subservient devotion to the military. That was Nazi Germany. In a free country such as the United States of America, scientists are allowed to form their own opinions. In a free country, scientists are allowed to exercise their own moral judgment."

"Even at the risk of national security? Delays in our hydrogen bomb program led to the Soviet's developing an H-bomb soon after ours."

"Maybe so," said Dad, "but it's good the Soviets have the super. It levels the playing field and therefore promotes world peace."

There were murmurs throughout the room as Mr. Goldfarb whispered to Dad.

"I've been advised by my counsel to strike that last comment from the record," said Dad. "Apparently promoting world peace is also being sympathetic to communism."

Shouts, whistles, and applause erupted from the room. Congressman Willis had to pound his gavel for order before the next question was asked.

"Do you believe in the sanctity of marriage?" asked another committee member.

"I do."

"Are you a bigamist, Dr. Kronenberger?"

"Yes, but that is the circumstance of being separated from my first wife during the war. It is not a communist plot."

I don't think Dad meant to be funny, but he sure was getting lots of laughs. If this was a circus as Mr. Goldfarb called it, Dad was stealing the show, which frustrated the committee.

"Is it true that your so-called 'circumstance of life' has driven Mrs. Shirley Kronenberger to a mental institution?"

Dad paused. His gaze fell upon me, and I mouthed the words, "Answer the question."

He released a long sigh. "My wife is in a hospital recuperating from a nervous breakdown, most likely caused by the hounding of this committee, the illegal FBI wire-tapping of our private telephone line, and the invasion and disruption of our personal lives."

"Do you believe children should be born into the protection of a legal marriage?"

Mr. Goldfarb leaned into the microphone. "It is outside the purview of this committee to inquire into—"

"The Chair will determine what is in the purview of this committee," said Congressman Willis.

"My rights as an American citizen are no less than those of Congress," argued Dad.

"You will have to answer the question, Dr. Kronenberger."

Dad turned to face me. We looked at each other for what seemed like a long time. I felt my head slowly turn to the right, then to the left.

"I will not answer the question," said Dad.

"Dr. Kronenberger, if you don't answer the question, you are in contempt of Congress," said Congressman Willis, "and if you are in contempt, you will leave the witness stand this instant."

Dad ran his hand up his sweaty brow and over his head. His voice was calm but steely. "If that contempt will facilitate the erosion of the credibility of this committee then it will be worth the cost."

Congressman Willis pounded his gavel. "Leave the witness stand."

"I will, gladly," said Dad. "For the sake my daughters, that they may grow and thrive in an America that upholds the Bill of Rights of the United States Constitution, which you are trampling with this outrageous hearing."

The gavel pounded louder and louder in an attempt to drown out Dad's words, but he'd been heard, loud and clear. Congressman Willis shouted into the microphone, "Officers, remove the witness."

Dad was pulled away from the microphone and escorted out by the police with Mr. Goldfarb following. I stared after them, stunned by what had just happened. At first it seemed I had given Dad courage to cooperate with Congress, but in the end, I was no help at all. I found my feet, stumbled over a row of people, and rushed out of the room to catch up with Dad and Mr. Goldfarb.

CHAPTER EIGHTEEN

Dad wore one of Mom's frilly aprons to make us laugh more than to protect his clothes. He had cleared out the spiders and cobwebs in our built-in brick barbeque, which hadn't been used in ages, and was now overseeing the steaks, sizzling on the grill. Alice sailed through the French doors bearing the potato salad above her head like a waiter in a fancy restaurant. She was clad in plaid pedal pushers and a mauve sweater set, her blond hair styled in a bouffant flip, which was becoming all the rage.

It was the evening before our departure for the family reunion in Guerneville. Alice wouldn't be accompanying us for the second year in a row. She claimed she had to read ahead since she was taking extra units in the fall, but I doubted that was the real reason. My parents seemed to understand why she would be shy about a big family gathering and didn't try to coax her along.

When we sat down to dinner on the patio, Dad thrust out his elbows as he enthusiastically attacked his steak. "How about those Giants?"

Mom leaned into Dad, her chin resting on her knuckle. She was pale and thin but she looked calm and rested. "What about those Giants?"

Dad reared back and his eyebrows shot up. "Three straight shut outs against the Dodgers. Can't beat that, darling."

Mom nodded toward the shelf of plants behind her. "Did you notice my African violets are blooming? Know my secret?"

"Do tell," said Dad.

Mom's lips quivered before she got the word out. "Coffee."

"You water them with coffee?" Dad asked.

"Not coffee..." Mom's mouth tensed. "What is it called—what's left over?"

"Grounds," offered Alice.

"Grounds," Mom repeated. "Donna, did you pack your car coat?"

"Aw, it's summer."

"It gets chilly in the evenings down by the river."

When everyone was done eating, I jumped up to clear the table.

"Who wants cobbler?" asked Mom. "I used fresh…oh, darn."

Alice laid her hand over Mom's and gently squeezed. "Give yourself a chance to think."

Mom shook her head. "Some words just don't come."

"They will eventually," said Alice. "Your speech is getting better every day. Isn't it, Daddy?"

"Peaches!" Mom exclaimed triumphantly. "Who wants peach cobbler?"

"None for me, thanks," said Alice, patting her belly that was nearly back to its normal flatness. "I've got to run. I'm meeting Darlene and some other students over on Telegraph to distribute Kennedy brochures."

"He's Catholic, Alice," said Dad. "This country won't allow a Catholic in the White House."

"Nothing wrong with trying. You voting for Nixon?"

Dad made a face like he had bitten into something rotten.

Alice chuckled. "That's what I thought."

"Kennedy's got my vote," said Mom. "He's so handsome!"

"Pooh, that's no reason to vote for him!" said Alice. "What about his New Frontier? Equal rights for everyone, Negroes, the poor, doesn't matter who you are."

"Pretty words, empty promises," said Dad.

Alice went behind him and put her arms around his neck. "You pessimistic old grump! We can't give up on the system now."

"Absolutely correct, sweetie." He kissed Alice's cheek.

I stabbed my peach cobbler with my fork as Alice and Dad continued to argue politics. Talk! Talk! Talk! Were we always going to jabber without saying what we really needed to say to each other? Wasn't anyone even going to acknowledge Alice had given birth? Wasn't anyone ever going to ask her how she felt about giving up her son?

Later that night, I lay on my bed reading while Alice sat at the desk. Her typewriter had been silent for several minutes. I caught her gazing vacantly across the room, something she often did, smoking one cigarette after another.

I slid down on my knees and pulled from between my mattress and springs her old notebook and all her other poems I had taken from the wastebasket. I smoothed the crumpled paper into a neat pile and set them and the notebook on the desk before her.

"What's all this?" she asked. "Why, you little sneak! You snooped through my trash!"

"Your poems! I saved them for you."

"Gee, thanks." She swiped them off the edge of the desk, causing them to land with a thump in the wastebasket. "Don't you know what it means when someone throws something away?"

"I don't see you writing poetry anymore. I thought if you read these, they might get you going again."

She took a long drag on her cigarette and let the smoke billow out her nostrils like a dragon. "The thing I want to write about, I can't, because it doesn't exist, dig? If I can't write what I want, there's no point in writing at all."

"Can't you at least talk about it to someone, like Darlene?"

"How can I talk about something that never happened?"

"Not even Darlene knows?"

"I'm not so close to Darlene anymore. I'm not like the other girls. I'm not like the beats. I don't fit in anywhere."

"You could talk…to me," I offered meekly.

"I'm especially not talking to you!"

I went back to my book. After a while, I set it aside, snuggled down in my bed and turned toward the wall. I listened to Alice getting ready for bed and waited for her to turn out the light before I spoke in a tiny voice, "I saw him."

She didn't reply. Finally, she let out a long sigh and murmured, "No, you didn't."

In Guerneville, same as at home, I kept track of what was not being said. Nothing was said about Mom's stay at Woodbridge. Nothing was said about Dad's HUAC hearing. Nothing was said about Alice's baby. I had to assume that none of my relatives knew about her pregnancy, but how was that possible? Mom couldn't even confide in her best friend in the world, Aunt Lillian? I thought how lonely secrets made people.

Gladys was talking though. "Donna called me in the dead of winter, long distance, just to see how I was. Wasn't that the sweetest thing?" We had to hear that several times.

The most fun I had at camp that year was one rainy afternoon when Chubby Checker came on the radio, singing "The Twist." I leaped up from my chair, singing along, "Come on, baby, let's do the twist!" I pivoted on the ball of my foot across the carpet until I got to where Dad was perched on the arm of the sofa.

When I pulled him to his feet, Uncle Howie exclaimed, "Easy, Donna, you'll throw the old man's back out."

Dad bent over and wiggled his bottom a little, which made everyone laugh.

"Put your hips into it, Daddy," I coached. "Twist!"

He mimicked my motions, pressing his hand in the small of his back, bearing a silly grin.

Cousin Tommy and his wife, Kathy, joined us. Tommy was really good, twisting down so that his bottom nearly touched the floor. Their two little daughters, Betsy and Susie, twisted together. Linda twisted with baby Charlie in her arms. Mom twisted, holding hands with Grandpa who remained seated in his big chair. Grandma clapped her hands to the beat. Even Gladys rose up on her crutches and swayed to the music.

Many things were left unsaid in Mom's large, extended family, but, at least, we could all twist together.

EPILOGUE

In the fall of 1960, I began my junior year in high school while my father went to prison to serve his sentence for contempt of Congress. Kennedy won the election in November, and although he claimed to be "tough on communism," HUAC seemed to fade away. There was something new and exciting about the Kennedys taking charge of the White House. Jackie was beautiful, Caroline and John-John were cute little kids, and there was lots of talk about outer space, culture, and prosperity.

Dad returned home at the end of February, having served only five months of his yearlong sentence. He resumed to his teaching duties at Cal fall semester as if he had been merely on sabbatical.

In March of the following year, Kennedy announced the inauguration of the Peace Corps, dubbed the "Kiddie Corps," because so many young people were eager to venture out in the world to make it a better place. Attending summer sessions and taking extra units each semester, Alice was able to graduate from Cal, at the end of the summer session in 1962. In October, she was shipped off to Nigeria, becoming one of the first Peace Corps volunteers. She not only found a place where she belonged; she found a use for her anthropology major. She never wrote another poem that I know of, but several years later she got a slim memoir published about her experiences in the fledging stages of the Peace Corps.

As for me, I graduated from Berkeley High School, class of 1962, and went on to the University of California, major undeclared. By then, change was in the air. The students weren't going to sit quietly in their classrooms, but clamored for Civil Rights and raged against the Vietnam War. Some of the protesters who made the most noise were the folk singers. Pete Seeger's "We Shall Overcome," Bob Dylan's "Blowin' in the Wind" and Peter, Paul, and Mary's "If I Had a Hammer" all topped the charts. There was even a song played in the coffee houses on Telegraph called "The Ballad of Leo Kronenberger," which claimed my father acted more American in insisting on his Constitutional rights than the House of Un-American Activities Committee who tried to take them away.

AUTHOR'S NOTE

In 1959, my father-in-law, James J. Lynch, was the University of California English professor who chaired the Subject A Committee, which was responsible for authoring examination essay questions for high school senior applicants. Of the twelve questions composed for that year, number seven, was the following: "What are the dangers to a democracy of a national police organization, like the FBI, which operates secretly and is unresponsive to public criticism?" The question and the ensuing controversy became the springboard of my novel, *Commie Pinko*.

Like my fictional character, Dr. Leopold Kronenberger, Professor Lynch and his committee were subjected to reprimand. Several high school seniors taking the exam complained that the question "assumed that the FBI was a danger to democracy," and the examination "was devised to weaken our resistance to orderly policing." Americanism Educational League executive director Dr. John R. Lechner became aware of the students' letters and requested that California Governor Edmund G. "Pat" Brown investigate the Subject A Committee. Brown referred the matter to the University of California Board of Regents.

After reviewing the situation, the Regents produced an open apology to the FBI. "The Regents of the University of California deeply regret that an improper question appeared on the Subject A exam that casts reflection on the Federal Bureau of Investigation. Steps are being taken to prevent a recurrence of a similar, unfortunate incident. The university has the highest respect for the FBI as an essential arm of the nation's security and of the rule of law which is the keystone of our democratic society." Professor Lynch and his committee, however, upheld their constitutional right of freedom of speech, claiming that the apology impaired the academic freedom of the Subject A Committee. Lynch pointed out that students did not have to choose question number seven, and, indeed, could take an opposing view of it. He further commented that "questions with 'shock value' cause students to write better essays in defense of beliefs that may otherwise be taken for granted."

Because of this controversy, the fall of 1959 and spring of 1960 was a stressful time for my husband's immediate family. My father-in-law kept a scrapbook of newspaper articles, letters-to-the-editor including the infamous one submitted by J. Edgar Hoover himself, and transcriptions of crank telephone calls he received. It was from this information that I gleaned direct quotes to use in my novel. The rest of my work, including characters and plot, is purely fictional and does not in any way represent members of the Lynch family.

One of my luckiest turns of fate is that I got to be married into this amazing, talented, and intelligent family. I would like to thank all my family, both the Nichols and the Lynch sides, my children, Caitlin and Sean, and all my friends for their support in my writing this novel. I am especially grateful to my husband, Tim, who acted as my in-house consultant and copy editor. I am indebted to my first readers, Barbara Kerr, Tanya Nichols, and Anne Frett, who offered their insight and valuable comments.

Printed in the United States
By Bookmasters